NEEDING YOU

The Carrington Chronicles

A. C. ARTHUR

AN ARTISTRY PUBLISHING BOOK

THE CARRINGTON CHRONICLES
NEEDING YOU
Copyright © 2014 by A.C. Arthur
First Edition: 2014
Print Edition: 2015

www.acarthur.net

Cover Design by Croco Designs
Interior format by The Killion Group
http://thekilliongroupinc.com

"I do not trust people who don't love themselves and yet tell me, "I love you." There is an African saying which is: Be careful when a naked person offers you a shirt."

~Maya Angelou

OTHER BOOKS BY A.C. ARTHUR

The Donovans & Donovan Friends
Love Me Like No Other
A Cinderella Affair
Guarding His Body
Defying Desire
Full House Seduction
Touch of Fate
Summer Heat
Winter Kisses
Holiday Hearts
Desire A Donovan
Surrender To A Donovan
Pleasured By A Donovan
Heart Of A Donovan
A Christmas Wish
Always My Valentine
Embraced By A Donovan

The Rules of the Game Trilogy
Rules of the Game
Revelations
Redemption

The Shadow Shifters
Temptation Rising
Shifter's Claim
Seduction's Shift
Hunger's Mate
Passion's Prey
Primal Heat – ***Coming August 4, 2015***

Wolf Mates
An Alpha's Woman – *Coming September 15, 2015*
www.acarthur.net

PROLOGUE

One Year Ago

I love to watch.

Yes, it's a little perverted and for this intolerable sin I'm probably two steps closer to my own personal room in Hell. Still it's a part of me, a full three lines in my daily itinerary. *WATCH JANA GETTING SCREWED.* That's what's scribbled in Monday evening's slot in big bold letters beneath *have dinner* and *feed Vicious.*

Unlike some others I've heard of, I don't watch for the thrill of being seen or getting caught. For me, it's totally different. I don't want to be caught or seen. I don't want anyone to know—especially my mother—that I enjoy sex. Well, I enjoy watching others have sex.

I was taught that sex was bad, that kissing, intimate touching, and its cohorts were evil. A sin in the face of God for which I could never repent.

At 28 years old, living on my own and working as a high school guidance counselor, you'd think I'd be over the sin and repent thing. Or at the very least that I'd have a better understanding of the whole philosophy. And actually, I do. For instance, I'm pretty sure my mother was a religious fanatic and that most of the crap she drilled into my head was her distorted adaptation of the Bible. She'd read that book so many times, dissecting it and reshaping it until it said what she needed it to say for her own peace of mind.

Once I'd escaped to college and had a chance to view the world on my own, I understood that much better. I also understood that sex might really be overrated. Only, I liked it on a certain level. At least I liked what I saw of it.

So, that's what I do. I watch.

I watch and I touch myself. I even finger fuck myself to the memory of watching.

I'm a Peeping Tom. Well, a Peeping Tomika. *No pun intended.*

But really, I don't mean to make light of my actions. It's an addiction, an obsession. I'm constantly curious if anyone knows that I'm watching. And if someone did know, what would they do? Would they welcome me? Would they stop, scream, run away? Would they have me arrested?

Thinking about all this is making me hot. It's a little after eight and he, Melvin, Jana's latest boyfriend, has just finished with his shower. I have a perfect view from my favorite black leather office chair situated approximately one foot from the window. My bedroom door is shut. The floor length charcoal gray drapes are tightly closed but for the small opening where my lens rests. I have one candle lit on the dresser across the room. It's scented. Lilac. I like the soft flowery aroma because it reminds me of hot summer days.

Melvin worked tonight down at the convenience store a couple of blocks away until his co-worker, the younger man with inky black curls, came in to relieve him. Melvin is a creature of habit. Jana knows this so she always has his dinner ready when he arrives. They sit in the small kitchen of Jana's house and eat together. Then Jana cleans the kitchen.

Jana works at a law firm for a couple of shady personal injury lawyers that she hates on bad days and loves on pay days. She's told me that hundreds of times in the years we've been neighbors. Her office is downtown and she's constantly moving about all day long with tasks like filing, delivering pleadings to the courts, picking up lunch and so forth. This doesn't sound the least bit exciting to me. Then again, counseling horny and hyper teenagers isn't always a walk in the park either.

I always arrive home before Jana and begin watching almost immediately, waiting. When Jana arrives she drops her purse and the black bag she carries her dress shoes and other work paraphernalia in onto the couch and heads to the kitchen.

Melvin arrives 45 minutes after Jana. She met him about two months ago. I began watching them about the same time.

Jana and Melvin fascinate me because they are totally uninhibited. They are young and absolutely absorbed with themselves. They have no fear of pushing the boundaries of their sexual relationship. Jana trusts Melvin to please her and Melvin does just that.

Of course it's strange that I'm still so damned afraid of recriminations from having sex, being touched by a man intimately—fornicating or living sinfully as my mother would say. It's even stranger that I'm hooked on watching other people enjoy sex to bring my own pleasure, but then my life has never been anything but strange. Besides, nobody knows that I watch and nobody knows that I pleasure myself. I don't even let Vicious, my adorable yet possessive bichon frisé, see.

So I am safe.

I adjust my chair making sure I'm in a comfortable position. It's an office chair, one that can recline at will. I concentrate on my telescope now. Some people think telescopes are only good for watching stars, planets and other such nonsense, but I have a more basic use. Still, the same way others want to see each star and hidden galaxy in perfect clarity, I want to see my lovers without any blurriness or distortion.

A year or so ago I bought a great reflecting telescope with a wide aperture. When you want to see something as if you're standing right in front of it, a reflecting telescope is the way to go. The wider the aperture the greater the resolution and magnification. The Dobsonian, that's the type of telescope I have, requires a lot of maintenance, but I don't mind. It's worth it.

I'm all set except my palms are sweating. Anticipation's a bitch. I've been thinking of Jana and Melvin all day. I'm horny as hell and need release like an alcoholic needs a drink.

I lick my lips, loving the feel of my moist tongue against the plump skin, willing my pulse to simmer down. They were finished eating dinner and Jana was in the bedroom waiting, just like me. Any minute now relief would come.

I have a clear view of the room. Jana likes bright colors, so the walls of her bedroom are canary yellow, the comforter on her bed red with numerous pillows in shades of yellow, purple and pink. That's something Jana and I have in common. We like pillows.

Jana moves to the dresser at the same time Melvin enters the room. I swallow quickly, my chest heaving, breasts tingling. Melvin walks up behind Jana, pulling her by the waist until her ass is aligned with his rigid dick. Melvin's dick is long and of medium width. He never shaves his groin, so his bushy brown hair surrounds an otherwise good looking shaft.

Jana's lips part in what looks like a sigh. She lets her head fall back onto his shoulder. I like the way her brown eyes grow dark with lust as her lips part. I imagine mine doing the same. One of Melvin's hands grasps her right tit and squeezes hard. I'm sucking air in huge gulps as my own hand grips my right breast.

He slips his other hand between her thighs, cupping her pussy. My clit jumps, standing at attention while my own walls spasm.

Jana is hot for him. I can tell because her nipples are pressing against the thin material of her shirt. I'm watching intently now as his fingers move over her juncture, pressing deeper against her pussy. His face is contorted, his motions rough, and I shiver because it's just the way I like it.

My pussy aches and I clench my thighs trying to get a handle on the whirlwind of sensations down there. I shift in the chair without taking my eyes off Jana and Melvin. He's swirling his tongue over her neck. Magnification through my finderscope is so good I can see the path of moisture he leaves on her skin. My breasts are heavy, in need of more attention, so I quickly drop my other hand from the slim nozzle of the scope. I'm now cupping both my breasts, kneading them with the same ferocious actions as Melvin.

Jana's mouth opens again and I swear I can hear her moaning. No, wait, that's me.

Melvin turns her to face him and quickly pulls her blouse over her head. Jana's not wearing a bra. Neither am I.

Melvin kneels down, taking her nipple between his teeth. Her head tilts back and for some reason Melvin shifts her so that now I have a side view. He's sucking her breast hungrily while squeezing the other globe until her nipple is turgid and red. I mimic his motions, feeling the intense spike of pain, and then the immediate flush of pleasure.

He pushes her pants down and stares at her anxiously while she steps out of them. Melvin is naked. Jana is naked. I am naked.

I wonder if he'll take her fast tonight or if he'll toy with her until she's screaming and begging for sweet release. I'm in the mood for fast and furious. I've waited all day, thinking about this, visualizing this. I need it *now*!

As if he hears my cries, Melvin lifts Jana. She wraps her legs around his waist and his long length slides into her glistening wet pussy.

Shit! I wasn't ready. I move the hand that was squeezing my breast to my pussy and plunge three fingers—because that's about how wide I measure Melvin to be—inside my juicy center. My body shakes uncontrollably as I keep my eye focused through the lens of the telescope.

Melvin is fucking Jana earnestly now and I move my fingers in and out with the same fevered motions. He's slamming into her pussy so hard her breasts are bouncing all over the place. I scoot to the edge of my chair and move until I feel my size C cups jiggling frantically too. Jana's mouth is open wider now and I know she's screaming, digging her nails into his back. He's calling her his dirty little slut and telling her how nice and hot her pussy is.

I know this because these are the words I want to hear.

I'm moaning now because my pussy is hot too. It's dripping wet and clutching my fingers. My hips are pumping against my hand as I feel my climax building anxiously.

"I'm gonna come."

I hear the words in my own voice but know that Jana is saying the same. Melvin's in rare form tonight, his muscled body moving furiously in and out of Jana. His face is contorted as if this act is causing him some sort of pain. That drives my desire higher and I shout out his name.

"You better fuckin' come!" Melvin's lips move and again I hear him saying what I want to hear.

I'm watching him closely now, how his ass cheeks grow taut with each thrust. He's got a great ass and strong muscled thighs. He's holding Jana up without breaking a sweat and he's plowing into her with no remorse. Jana's legs are wrapped tightly around him, but when I move the telescope a fraction of an inch I can see his balls slapping against her pussy lips and a tiny glimmer of Jana's flowing juices.

I'm breathing heavily now, wanting to come at the same time that they do. I rub my thumb over my clit, clenching my teeth with the glorious sensations rippling through me. I love this feeling, this building that soars through me, starting as a pulse in my pussy, then moving with warm persistence up toward my stomach.

It's swirling through me now like a tornado. I'm caught in the funnel of pleasure, feeling the haze of euphoria envelop me. It's great, this intense rush of gratification. My fingers are going deeper, stretching my center before finding my spot. I tilt my fingers a bit and rub. My entire body trembles and I clench my teeth.

"Oh God," I whimper, helpless to the onslaught of sensations about to overcome me.

My fingers continue to move, my hips gyrating against them. It's coming. It's coming. I can feel it coming.

Jana's mouth opens, her head tilting back and I scream as loud as I ever have with our release. Melvin yells as his seed pours into her. I imagine its warmth being injected in me as well.

My moan is low and soul deep, coming from a place in me that I keep hidden from the world. Seconds later

I'm humming as my fingers still, feeling the contraction of my pussy walls and the hot release of my climax. I squeeze my thighs tightly together, still humming and biting my bottom lip riding on this delicious wave of satiation.

I lean back in my chair, my eyes closed as I try to come down from this magnificent high. I am so relaxed, my limbs are loose and languid. I'm ready for bed. Well, a quick shower first and then bed. Maybe I'll read that new suspense novel I bought or watch...

My spine tingles. The heat that had just engulfed me is replaced by a cold draft. I sit up in the chair once more and out of habit lean forward to look through the lens. Jana's mouth is open again, as if she's screaming, similar to how she had moments ago when we'd come. Only this time I'm almost positive there's more pain than pleasure. Her eyes aren't hazy with lust anymore but glazed frozen with shock.

With a vicious swing of his arm, Melvin slashes a deadly blade with a sinister silver gleam over Jana's torso. Blood spews from her chest in a spray of crimson, landing on the red comforter. He repeats this motion until wide arcs of blood splatter against the bright canary walls like an artist creating an abstract work of art.

Jana's features are frozen as he cuts through her skin. Blood is everywhere now, leaking from every conceivable hole in her body. In my mind there are screams, in my body icy pain that steals my breath.

I can't move. Nor can I think beyond what I'm seeing.

He's killing her.

Melvin, the man with the long dick who fucked my neighbor the way I secretly wanted to be fucked is committing murder. And I'm sitting in my chair, my pussy still damp with my release, my heart beating rapidly, watching him do it.

CHAPTER ONE

"Tell me how you really feel."

Jack paused the moment he heard those words, in that voice. It was the voice he'd waited all week long to hear. The one that called to him even as he sat in his office staring out the window to the evening sky, knowing he should be heading home, but not wanting to go from one room where he sat alone, to another. It was an eerie feeling, one which he was not accustomed to, one that he did not like.

Adonna always wanted to know how he felt and then how he wanted to feel. All he had to do was tell her and she would oblige.

But he never did.

"We have an hour and then I must leave," had been his staunch reply.

He was in the Sunset Room, his personal suite at the elite sex club called The Corporation, located in a high rise building in Beverly Hills. The Corporation had facilities all over the world, its clientele reaching as high up as White House staff to as low as businessman daring to pay the required huge sum of money and risk the demise of all they'd built in their professional lives for the pleasure that drove everything they did, everything they could ever imagine.

Membership at The Corporation was a powerful drug, taking money from the globe's largest bank accounts to fund an age-old habit. An enterprise built by men and women with one thought in mind: pleasure. The idea had been simple, its implementation professional and high class, its profits, overwhelming. And as a 40% shareholder, Jackson Carrington reaped the rewards for all ends.

On a more socially acceptable level, Jack's other position was CEO of Carrington Enterprises. His annual salary, coupled with a trust fund his grandfather had set up for him and his two younger brothers before his death, made him one of the top five richest men in the world. With this title came a few more amenities, such as social prestige and enhanced financial stability. More frequently, however, this title hampered him with family obligation, unsolicited high-profile attention, and the sour taste of dishonesty that recently burned like acid through his conscientiousness.

"How would you like to feel tonight, sir?"

She liked calling him sir. Jack could take it or leave it, but figured as far as endearments went that it was best to keep it clear as day where everyone in this particular room stood.

Today, of all days, that was a loaded question. So much had happened this week that he didn't quite know where to begin. Oh, yes he did. He unbuttoned his shirt, hanging it on one of the bed's four posts, giving her a full show as he removed the gold cufflinks and set them on the bedside table. Pulling his undershirt from his pants, he lifted it up and over his head before draping it over the same post that held his shirt. He could feel the heat on his skin as her eyes bore into his naked chest. He sat on the side of the bed and untied his Burberry suede brogues, removed them, setting them neatly in front of the bedside table. He stood once more, his hands immediately going to the gold buckle of his belt. Slipping the button from his pleated navy blue dress slacks and pulling slowly on the zipper, he watched with immeasurable pleasure as she licked her lips, the professional demeanor she always put forth slipping slowly but surely.

When he pushed the pants down his thighs to step out of them one leg at a time, he heard her sharp intake of breath. Jackson folded his pants neatly on the pleat, taking a few steps across the room to drape them over the chair that matched the cherry wood desk near the door. Turning back to her, he removed his boxers. He didn't move slow, didn't prolong the inevitable, but just took care of the deed, until he was standing directly in front of her, naked.

"I don't want to feel anything," was his reply.

It was always the same. If he felt anything, he could easily regret it. If he regretted coming to The Corporation, he would without a doubt stop coming. If he stopped coming, his life, the one part of it he could safely say he owned, would be over.

When she stood, it was with a smile and a practiced seduction that Jack had appreciated instantly upon meeting her. Tonight she would give him what he needed—nothing more and certainly nothing less. That was the way it worked, at least for him. Business first, then family and then his indulgences. Happiness, contentment and peace were all overrated.

Jack closed his eyes then and waited for the pleasure, for the thick fog that coming here always entrenched him in. It wasn't quite euphoria but he thought it might be as close as he would ever get. Her fingers were all over his body, seemingly at once. At his shoulders, down the back of his tight ass, over his thighs. She may have been naked by now as well, but Jack didn't see. He couldn't see that much, couldn't focus on anything beyond that haze, the comfort zone he'd allowed this place to become.

The warmth that engulfed him the second her mouth wrapped around his dick caused his body to shake, his spine tingling with pleasure spikes reaching up, up, until a heavy breath whooshed from his lips. At his sides his fingers clenched. He didn't touch her. Had never needed to put his hands on her.

An echo sounded in his ears, like ocean waves lifting and crashing, as she took him deep, sucked him hard. His hips jutted forward in one shallow pump. She grabbed his toned buttocks, a request for more. Jack gave it to her. He gave all the pent up frustration from his week at work, all the family drama he hadn't wanted to be part of but was unfortunately engrossed in just the same. He pumped into her mouth without mercy, without conscious thought of whether he should or shouldn't. He could and so he did, over and over until his release finally burst free in jetted pulses that tugged at everything swirling around inside of him. Everything he wanted desperately to ignore.

When she was finished, when swallowing came as natural as her next breath, Jack walked to the bed and took a seat. He lay back without the necessity of a pillow and waited the few moments it would take for her to follow him, sheath his throbbing length with a condom, climb atop him and position herself the way he liked. Through half opened eyes he could see her slender back, the line of her spine and the curve of her hips. Her hair was short, curving around her neck in what may have been soft auburn wisps. She spread her legs wide, squatting over him while her hand grasped his still hardened cock. Lowering herself slowly she pressed the bulging head of his erection into her deliciously wet pussy.

Jack didn't move, didn't bother to help the process along. He liked it almost tortuously slow sometimes, mostly when his mind was too full of other bullshit to instruct anything else.

Adonna liked the performance, liked to show him how well suited she was for this job.

When she'd completely swallowed him inside the tight heated walls of her pussy, Jack gritted his teeth, wanting the next release to be powerful enough, potent enough to wipe the slate clean, to get him ready for the next day. Otherwise he wasn't sure he'd make it, wasn't even positive he wanted to.

Today was the day.

The first day of the rest of her life—or rather the start of Tara Sullivan's life. Melanie Morgan's life had effectively died the moment Melvin Corone's knife ripped through Jana's skin. She could think about it now—a year later—and not break out into a sweat, shaking and mumbling incoherently until she was given those freaking anxiety meds that made her nauseous just before putting her in a coma-like slumber for the next twenty-four hours. A couple of times she'd even faked the attack just to get the meds and have an excuse to lay in bed, eyes closed, mind blank, not caring to live another moment.

But she did need to live. She needed to get out of this house and breathe something more than this Pacific Ocean air. As a result of all the time she'd been denied, her need was stronger now than it had ever been before. And regardless of all that she'd been through, she needed to move on.

Two weeks ago she'd testified in one of the biggest federal organized crime trials of the century. For three days she'd talked, putting the details of her entire life— Melanie Morgan's life—on display for twelve jurors and four alternates to dissect. They'd looked at her as if she was tainted, possessed by some unholy element as she'd explained how she came to witness the murder. Yet she hadn't faltered. There had been no breakdown, no tears and no regrets, only a rigid distance she'd learned to keep between herself and the world so long ago.

When the trial was over, she'd felt a modicum of relief. The marshals who had become her roommates and only friends (acquaintances might be a better word) for the past year had moved out days after she'd returned to Seal Beach. Once again alone, the urges had kicked in full force, as if that part of her would not be erased by the FBI or all their ingenious efforts to create a new identity and life for her, for Tara Sullivan.

Her hands shook as she fastened the gold chain link necklace around her neck, words echoing in her head, scolding and reprimanding before either were technically needed.

Now the works of the flesh are evident: sexual immorality, impurity, sensuality, idolatry, sorcery, enmity, strife, jealousy, fits of anger, rivalries, dissensions, divisions, envy, drunkenness, orgies and things like these. I warn you, as I warned you before…

Doris Leigh Morgan had warned Melanie every day of the 17 years they'd resided together. In the small house in Syracuse where they'd resided, Doris Leigh upheld what she considered the purest and most devout life they could have in the sinful world that surrounded mother and daughter. Melanie had been raised to worship her body as a temple and to never, ever let anyone invade that temple. Doris Leigh didn't even believe in the institute of marriage, which could have been because the man that had impregnated and promised to marry her had disappeared before the third trimester of that pregnancy had come to an end. To say

Melanie had been raised by a bitter, intolerant Bible-spouting mother would have been a severe understatement.

It was also her biggest inspiration. After all, if not for the way she was raised, Melanie would have never found the one ultimate form of release that made her feel as high as any controlled substance and as free as any other revelation could.

It seemed like only yesterday she'd been heading off to work at Benjamin Lewton High School, sitting behind the old ragged desk in the small office with no window, shuffling through school records and college preparatory brochures. Her job as a guidance counselor had been ideal in that she worked in a place where there was no need for her to be attractive or seductive because she was surrounded by teenagers. Jana had scoffed at that notion, saying it was a waste of her intelligence and her time. But she'd liked it. She'd liked it a lot. And now it was gone. She could never return to Dalton, the small upstate New York town she'd lived in since graduating from college, nor return to Brewton High School and the students that had given her a reason to live.

They'd come to her house, the 1970s split level that had been her first major purchase after college, the one directly across from another split level, a little more updated than hers, that Jana had lived in. Dressed in dark suits, flashing badges that glistened in the early morning sunshine, they barely greeted her before stepping quickly inside without invitation.

"U.S. Marshals," the tall, broad shouldered one with sandy brown hair had said immediately. "We're here to get you moved."

In the next 15 minutes, it had been explained that Melvin was connected to Fernando Penelli, the head of one of only five remaining American/Italian families that formed the La Cosa Nostra, or as they were more commonly known, the American branch of the Italian Mafia. The marshal continued on to say that Melvin, known to the FBI as Big Mel, was a hit man for Penelli. Just three weeks prior to killing Jana, Big Mel had allegedly killed club owner Vladimir Pajari and his wife Irina in their Park Avenue penthouse. They didn't have enough evidence to bring Big Mel in on the Pajari murders, but with Melanie's eyewitness testimony they had him solidly connected to Jana's.

Which now made her a target for a Mafia hit.

She'd sat in her kitchen, numb to every other emotion except fear. It had a death grip on her, tightening around her neck until she could barely speak.

"You want me to go into hiding until it's time to testify?" she'd asked, her voice surprisingly not cracking even once.

"Yes, we want to keep you alive until you testify," the bigger, broader built guy said.

The other guy, a slightly slimmer one with a much better looking suit on, had knelt beside her, taking one of her hands in his. He'd looked directly into her eyes. His were a piercing blue, his hair trimmed shorter on the sides, laying neatly like a raven's wing. Normally she didn't like to be touched, especially by men she didn't know, but she hadn't made any attempt to take her hand from his, had only stared into his eyes instead.

"It's our job to keep you alive, period," he'd told her. "I'm Emilio Alvarez and I'll be in charge of getting you moved and settled into your new identity."

She'd frowned, felt her forehead furrow, eyes narrowing. "New identity?"

"Yes. You will leave this place and everything that Melanie Morgan was behind you. Tomorrow you'll be someone else, living somewhere else and you'll be safe," Emilio told her.

She looked to the other one, who had taken on a stone-like silence, his angry gaze aimed toward Emilio now.

"We've got 15 minutes," he told both of them sternly. "Get whatever you want to take and let's go."

Before she could even register moving through her house grabbing the pictures she'd wanted, her clothes, her box of private papers and Vicious—Emilio was nice enough to grab Vicious' cage and doggie treats—she was seated in the back of a black van heading to who knows where with men she prayed were who they said they were. It hadn't occurred to her to ask for credentials and really, she wouldn't have known if those credentials were real or fake if she had. Nothing like this had ever happened to her before, nothing had been so serious, so deadly, and as she clutched a shaking Vicious close to her chest she'd wondered exactly what tomorrow and this "someone else, living somewhere else" would bring.

It brought Tara Sullivan to Seal Beach, California, where she would slowly transition into a citizen once more. Slowly being the operative word since after the first two months of feeling sorry for herself and missing everything she'd left behind, she'd finally focused enough to start her own graphic design business. Within six months, her client list consisted of 30 authors and publishers. With the help of software she'd learned how to use from one of her students at the high school, she'd become well known in the literary industry, designing the hottest book covers and advertising materials. The money she'd made in the first months of business, combined with the proceeds from the sale of her first house, had afforded her the down payment to her new home.

After she'd agreed to testify for the prosecution, Emilio had given her the rundown of how the WITSEC program worked. The marshals would protect, house and feed her until the trial was over and Melvin was safely behind bars. Once that happened, she would be on her own as Ms. Tara Sullivan, resident of Seal Beach, owner of Vicious Designs. At 29 years old, she would be a new woman with a new house, new career and the same old urges that had gotten her into this predicament in the first place.

According to Emilio, she'd been one of the best witnesses he'd ever had to relocate. Because she'd had no living family and no close friends, the threat of her calling someone from New York or wanting to someday go back was slim. She'd never complained or cried, only went with the flow of things. What other choice did she have? She could live or she could die.

She chose to live.

And tonight, that choice would evolve. She would be the woman she'd never had the guts to be when she was Melanie Morgan. She would reach out and grab the things that Jana had told her were so worthwhile, so worth taking the risk for. Tara would be everything Jana had showed her she could be, and more.

She pulled her now long wavy hair up into a neat bun and slipped a black blazer over the sleeveless hot pink dress she wore and prepared to leave her pretty little yellow house on the corner of a road aptly named Sunnydale. Vicious, her adorable puppy and best friend in the entire world, looked up at Tara expectantly with her big black eyes, wagging her fluffy white tail.

"You'll be fine," she told her, but Vicious didn't look convinced.

"I'll be fine, too," Tara said with a huff as she made sure Vicious' water bowl was full. "I know they're gone. But it's just as well. Russ hated his job and he hated me. He never even came into the house anyway. And Emilio said we could call him if anything out of the ordinary happened. I've got his cell number programmed in my phone. And Melvin is in jail. We'll be fine." The last sentence was stated in a voice a little softer than before as she looked around.

"I won't be gone long. I promise," she told Vicious, who she could swear was giving her the most sorrowful look ever to grace a dog. She sighed. "I just have to do this. I know you don't understand. You never did. Jana understood. She knew why I needed this, why I had to do this my way."

At the memory, tears welled in her eyes and Tara gave in to the moment of grief. She leaned against the white tile countertop with its lovely blue floral design that had made her fall in love with this beach house in the first place. "Jana knew everything about me and now there's nobody. Nobody who knows me and why I am...the way I am."

Vicious had become the only person she could talk to, even though she wasn't a person at all. Jana had always listened to her, always knew just what to say to talk her down off the ledge, to make her see that life was worth living. Now that she was gone, there was a small part of Tara that remained afraid. Luckily another part of her, the newer, bolder part that had allowed her to speak loud and clear on that witness stand, was calling for her to take another step. It was pushing her to move on with her life, to keep forging forward or else let Jana's death be in vain.

With determined strides, Tara refused to allow that happen. She walked through the cheerfully outfitted kitchen into her living room, which she was still in the process of decorating, and to the front door. Without looking back she opened the door. The alarm system she'd paid a small fortune to have installed beeped immediately, announcing that the front door had been opened. She had thirty seconds to enter in the code that would bypass the alarm before it sent a message to the local law authorities. She punched in the code and then closed and locked the door behind her, knowing the alarm system would automatically reset itself the moment the locks clicked back into place.

Right in front of her house sat the cab she'd requested through an online reservation a half hour ago. For a moment she paused because she was not used to stepping out of her house alone. When they'd taken her out to travel to New York for the trial, Emilio had walked right beside her, two other marshals dressed in black suits to her left and behind her. Russ, with his always scowling face, had stood by the truck, watching and waiting.

Tara swallowed as she looked across the street to the spot where Russ' truck was usually parked. He rarely came into her house, preferring to do his job from a distance, she supposed. Tonight, he was not there.

Blinking away the instant trepidation, Tara walked to the cab. She slipped into the backseat and gave the driver the address to where she wanted to go.

"987651 Wilshire Boulevard," she stated softly.

Sitting back against the worn leather seats, Tara stared out the window, her mind wandering to what she was doing, what she expected to get out of this little outing and how relieved she was going to feel when she woke up tomorrow. She thought about how finding that business card tucked in one of the only purses she'd had a chance to take with her when she'd moved was like a sign. Jana had always believed in signs. She'd said it was God's way of guiding people who had a phobia against the Bible. Tara had laughed at that since she'd never been able to open a Bible and read it thanks to her mother's obsession with quoting every sentence she could from the holy book.

She fingered the card with its embossed gold and black lettering. THE CORPORATION was all it said, a website address on the back. Her heart hammered as she remembered the last time she'd been to The Corporation, the last time she'd been able to see all the pleasure her body could withstand. That's what she wanted tonight, that's what she craved—the pleasure, the soul shattering, eye-opening shards of pure bliss that sliced through her each time she blinked her eyes, each time she watched.

CHAPTER TWO

Jack had showered and slipped back into his slacks and dress shirt. His jacket and tie remained in the room while he walked the lower level of the club. Each of The Corporation facilities he'd visited—New York, Miami, Chicago and Turks and Caicos—had different themed décor, all stately and exquisitely done. Beverly Hills was his home location and this layout he knew very well. The property had an old law firm feel with its heavy dark oak furniture, rich mahogany painted walls and plush forest green carpet. From one room to the next, some separated by heavy marble columns, others by dark brown shutter doors, there was an air of money and privilege thickly layered over the foundation of sexual pleasure and fantasies.

It smelled of new leather throughout the facility. Contracted employees such as Adonna were dressed in black suits, and male and female staff were clad in white pants and shirts and red ties, moving around unobtrusively. There were a few new faces tonight, probably guests of other members. None of them would stop and hold conversations, asking about each other's day or how their work was going. That wasn't the purpose of being here. This wasn't a personal club of friends or a network of any kind, at least not for Jack.

Still, as he looked around, he could admit feeling more at home here than any other place in the world.

The first floor of The Corporation was set up like one big lounge, each room fitted with deep cushioned leather chairs, sturdy wooden side tables and Persian rug overlays. Some spaces had floor-to-ceiling windows looking out over the city of the rich and famous. Drinks were provided to each member without the necessity of the member placing an order. The staff at The Corporation had an extensive file on each of their members. Employees knew what guests liked, what they disliked and what they would probably pay extra for before the member even stepped through the door.

Jack sat in a corner chair in the third room from the front entrance. This room always had the least amount of people occupying it at one time because it only had six chairs, all centrally located so that the view through the windows could be enjoyed by all. Recessed lighting kept the room just dim enough that identification was possible, but dark enough still that if one wanted to touch or taste, they were offered a measure of privacy.

"Your drink, Mr. Carrington," Tavena announced, bending slightly forward, offering his preferred vodka and cranberry.

"Thank you, Tavena," he replied, taking the glass and giving her a smile.

Unlike some of the board members, Jack was always cordial to everyone at The Corporation, especially the staff. He knew that the level of confidentiality expected from the club came with an even higher price tag than a member's annual dues could cover. While The Corporation had a very low rate of, and even lower tolerance of, staff members talking about what went on here, Jack was of the notion that it was wiser to be extra safe than sorry. He applied the same philosophy in all his business practices—Jack was cordial, professional and appreciative until he was given a reason not to be. So even though it wasn't required of him, he tipped well and conversed with the staff as if they were part of his family, or at least very close neighbors.

This could also be viewed as self-preservation on his part. The last thing Jackson Carrington, CEO of Carrington Enterprises and one of Beverly Hills' most powerful businessmen needed, was for news of his involvement with The Corporation to be leaked. His parents would be devastated, his brothers and their business endeavors undoubtedly affected, and the life he'd been born to lead, destroyed.

Jack did not take any of those things lightly, not for one minute.

Lifting the glass to his lips for his first sip, he stared out the window, thinking of the double life he'd led for as long as he could remember. As important as he knew it was to keep this part of himself concealed, the weight of the lies and secrets he'd been telling were beginning to take their toll. All day long he'd been in meetings, hammering out the final offer to take over a shipping company based in New England and avoiding the numerous text messages from his mother asking when he would be available for their annual summer get together. The Carringtons were a close-knit family, he and his two younger brothers being the light of their parents' lives since they'd both taken on full time retirement. The campaign for good, solid marriages and grandchildren had been in full swing since his youngest brother Jason married Celise Markam, successfully merging Jason's Carrington Resorts with Markham Inns and Suites. Yet, as happy as Jack was for his youngest brother, he wasn't about to be the next to take the fall.

The cool vodka mixture was making its way down his throat as Jack once again held the glass to his lips and coughed. Sitting up straight to keep from totally choking on his drink, his gaze fixated on the window— no, on the woman's reflection he could clearly see in the window. Lowering his glass, he turned slightly in his seat looking across the room only to have something get caught in his throat again. He coughed once more, this time using his free hand to cover his mouth and muffle the sound. All the while his gaze remained fastened on her.

Jack had seen her before. Hell, he'd tasted her before—the kiss that had haunted him for the last year since he closed the deal on that Manhattan-based communication's company. It had been a night just like this one, a Friday night, and he'd been at the New York branch of The Corporation.

He was up out of the chair before he could take another sip, another breath. As if he'd called out to her, she stopped the moment he stood, turning and looking directly at him. Again.

Breathing evenly was becoming more difficult with each step Tara took. She'd been excited when she stepped out of the cab in front of the tall building, every nerve in her body on end as anticipation of what lay ahead buzzed throughout her system. On the elevator ride up she'd licked her lips repeatedly, ready for the evening that would hopefully remove so much of the tension that had built over the past ten months like a damn about to break.

She needed this, she reminded herself. Needed it like she needed the air to breathe. All these months she'd been suffocating, sitting alone in that house or the previous cottage that they'd kept her in, with only the occasional marshal caring enough or being bored enough to sit down and talk to her about current affairs. Grief still cloaked her, affording minimal reprieve through the bouts of crying and regret. What insignificant human interaction she was afforded before the trial had not been enough. And when she'd tried to log in to any of the sites online that would provide her at least a semblance of relief, it was only to find that they'd all been blocked, no doubt courtesy of the very protective half of her marshal detail—Emilio—who would probably be fired on the spot if any of Penelli's men were smart enough to reach out to her via the uncontrollable sexual urges she practiced.

Her palms were sweating and she eased them down the front of her dress, over thighs that tingled with the contact. Every part of her body was extra sensitive, so eager for relief she almost couldn't stand it a second longer. Except now the anticipation had been joined by the shock waves of fear that always engulfed her whenever she was out in public, about to do what she needed to do. It was the stress of others watching her and possibly knowing she had a penchant for watching them.

Flee from sexual immorality. Every other sin a person commits is outside the body, but the sexually immoral person sins against his own body.

She knew that one by heart, had heard her mother say it so many times, when Melanie woke up in the morning and just before she left for school and again when she came home in the afternoon. Sometimes Doris Leigh would even stand in the doorway of Melanie's bedroom and whisper them while she thought Melanie was sleeping, as though she wanted the Bible verses programmed into her daughter like the ultimate stop sign, keeping her away from men now and forever.

Away from sex was more like it, and any and all things that came along with it.

Leave. Leave now and be saved.

That was her own voice, or rather the voice of Melanie, the one she'd left behind.

No! Tara refused. She was no longer Melanie, no longer that scared and confused woman who wanted to straddle the fence of being the good girl as her mother wanted and depriving the sexual being that lived deep inside of her. Squaring her shoulders, she turned completely away from the door and the exit that was calling to her. What faced her on the other side was a cornucopia of sensations, scents and emotions. Straight ahead were two men and a woman, a picture of what could've been a professional conversation in another space. The woman wore a dress that hung just past her knees, purple with a thick silver belt at her waist. The men both wore dark suits and ties. They seemed to be only talking, and yet the circle they were in was a little closer than normal, a tad more intimate than a professional chat. When one man's hand cupped the woman's cheek, tilting her head so that her open lips were close enough for him to lick, a tingle slithered down Tara's spine. The second man, standing behind the woman, reached down, and Tara thought he may have dropped something on the floor or possibly felt uncomfortable being so close and watching the other two play tongue hockey out in the open. But no, his hand slipped through a split in the side of the woman's dress, one that appeared to stretch upward to her thigh. She wore a black garter and the man's fingers toyed with the clasp before disappearing between her legs.

Tara's breasts swelled, her mouth watering at the sight. From behind someone bumped into her.

"Excuse me," said a woman, clad in slim black pants, a white shirt and red tie.

"No problem," Tara mumbled, stepping out of the woman's path and ending up inside a room she'd noticed on her left before the threesome had snatched her attention.

It was darker in here. Lamps with small golden shades were centrally located on heavy wood tables in each corner. There were large leather chairs with wide arms and high backs, eight of them throughout. Along the far wall were windows, floor-to-ceiling, the Beverly Hills skyline visible even through the dark tint. It felt warmer in here than it had been just in the hallway. A trickle of sweat slid slowly, sensuously between her sensitive breasts.

There were no couples in here, only three men, each sitting in a chair, each...staring at her. Her heart stuttered at that realization and she looked at the closest man as he sat legs spread wide, one thick fingered hand caressing his engorged dick. Looking away from him quickly, there was another man who simply stared at her as if trying to figure out if she were worthy. He reminded her of Russ and she turned her head from him instantly. The third man was holding a drink in his hand, staring at her, beckoning her with his eyes only.

Immediately she felt hotter, a funnel of warmth starting at the bottom of her stomach rising with a powerful twist until she felt like she would choke right then and there. He didn't speak but she knew he wanted her to come closer. He hadn't moved a muscle since she'd entered this room, and yet she felt inexplicably drawn to him. She took a tentative step because she had no idea what else to do, but then froze, as if her mind had suddenly taken a hint as to what might be about to happen.

Seconds ticked by with the man not moving and her not moving—a standoff. Tara had never felt so exposed in her life. Sure, she was standing in the center of this room fully dressed in an establishment where she was sure there were a good number of other people unclad.

But as these three men looked at her, watched her, she felt like they might possibly see everything there was inside. The girl that had been taught to hate men and sex, the young woman who had retreated into watching instead of doing, the woman who had watched her best friend get fucked and murdered.

Shaking now, she turned, knowing she had to go, hating the realization but fearing a complete breakdown if she didn't get some fresh air and out of the line of sight.

She'd just managed to turn around and was about to take another step when she felt his arm wrap around her waist. Without even blinking she knew exactly which man it was because her body reacted instantly to his touch, the same way it had when their gazes had connected. Arousal coated her vulva lips, dampening the thin slip of lace serving as her underwear. Her nipples tingled, hardened, and she gave an inaudible gasp.

Run! Run for your life!

A strange, urgent thought that had her heart pounding while her body remained still.

"It's good to see you again," he whispered, the hard length of his body pressed against hers.

His voice was deep, smooth, like a professional voice actor performing a commercial for anything pleasurable, anything at all that she would quite possibly purchase just from hearing him. She blinked, trying to keep her composure and knees from buckling.

"Hello," was her tentative reply.

Then, as his words replayed in her mind, Tara turned to look at him. "Did you say again?"

The left corner of his mouth lifted into a half smile, his already dark eyes going even darker as they narrowed slightly.

"You didn't think I could forget you, did you?" he asked, taking another step so that his scent was all she could smell. Fresh, male, potent as hell.

Tara took a step back. "I don't know you," she said slowly, realizing just at that moment the dangerous situation she was in.

Not only was this gorgeous, muscled man looking at her as if he were seriously considering picking her up, wrapping her legs around his waist and fucking her right here in this room, but he was acting as if he already knew who she was. Only, Tara wasn't anybody that a man like this should know. In fact, nobody besides the Social Security Administration, the federal government and her mortgage company had any idea who Tara Sullivan was.

So if he knew her, that meant...she turned to leave, fear holding her firmly in its grip. Not of herself or her needs this time, but of the fact that she'd been foolish enough to leave the safety of her house in Seal Beach and the luxury of having a marshal just one phone call away for protection.

His fingers wrapped around her arm, halting her steps, and she opened her mouth to scream. But when he turned her into him, his lips crashed down over hers before any sound could be released.

Warmth flooded quickly throughout her body as his tongue plunged inside her mouth without hesitation. Her eyes fluttered, hands poised against his shoulders to attempt pushing him away. Instead Tara found herself cocooned by his strong arms, flushed in a swirl of desire that made her head spin, her mind clear of all coherent thoughts and worries. His lips moved expertly over hers, taking the kiss deeper, making her want more.

When his hands flattened on her back, pressing her closer to him until her breasts rubbed seductively against his hard and toned chest, she moaned. She heard it, even above the rampant beating of her heart and the warning that continued to run on loop in the back of her mind. Her nipples hardened, her pussy clenching until she tightened her thighs to hold the growing pressure at bay.

Her fingers uncurled, straightening over the material of his shirt, feeling, for the first time ever in her life, strength exuding from a man. She squeezed, letting the duel between their tongues continue. Inhaling through her nose she let the smell of him mingle with the feel of him and she thought, maybe, just maybe, she could enjoy this. Maybe she didn't have to just watch, not this time, not in this new life. She could do more, be more, have more…and oh yes, she wanted more of him.

That was until his hands moved to her bottom, pressing her into what felt like endless inches of thick, long erection. Scenes flashed through her mind like a bad movie trailer with no sound. On and on, some moving faster than others: Melvin's erection as he speared into Jana. Jana's mouth open wide as she probably yelled Melvin's name, the pleasure so intense. And then the pleasure ended. And there was only pain—a deep dark pain that resonated throughout Tara's body, causing her to shake uncontrollably and to finally pull away from his embrace.

For a few seconds that felt like a millennia, he only stared at her, his brow furrowed in confusion. Her fingers—the ones that had just been touching him— shook as she lifted them to touch her still damp lips. When her legs began to shake, Tara knew she had to get out of there before she made a complete fool of herself. She took a few steps back, not sure about turning her back to him, possibly leaving and never seeing him again. That was a stupid sensation, a thought that never should have filtered into her mind because, hell, she had no idea who this man was. And yet...he was still looking at her as if he knew her, and now in a more intimate way.

She turned then, the word "run" blasting throughout her mind like someone was shouting it through a bullhorn. But she only made it as far as the elevator before she had to stop, slapping her palm against the button already glowing on the wall.

Stupid, stupid, stupid, she chastised herself. She should have stayed in the house. Should have continued to harbor in that shelter, even if the trial was over and the threat against her life now lifted. She should have never thought she could live on her own here, without Jana.

She was beyond stupid! And this damned elevator was beyond slow!

When the doors finally opened, dark oak doors that looked like the rest of the walls in this place, she all but ran inside, pressing the button designated for the lobby insistently. Finally, she moved all the way to the back, letting her head fall against the wall, watching through half-closed eyes as the doors began to close.

Then they opened again and he stepped inside.

It was like all the air had been sucked out of the enclosure and Tara gasped as she stood up straight, still huddling in the corner.

"Didn't take you for a runner," he said once the doors had closed behind him.

In this light, she could see the tight ebony curls of hair at the top of his head, the closer cut along the sides. His beard and mustache were neatly cut equally as close, adding an edgy frame to his dark eyes and serious gaze. His slacks were a dark gray, his shoes, shiny tie-ups, and his shirt white. All was too much and too close and she didn't know how to handle it.

"I shouldn't be here," she said. "I shouldn't have come."

One of his brows arched as he slipped his hands into his pockets. "Did you come all the way from New York just to see me?"

"What? Who are you?" she asked, fear clogging in her throat, even though she figured he wasn't a contract killer because the perfect time to finish her off would have been before the elevator doors opened again. They were almost to the bottom floor and he looked pretty damn casual—and sexy—standing there questioning her.

"Jackson Carrington," he said as though the name should have meant something to her. It didn't, but she thought it might be best not to vocalize that at the moment.

"Ah, no, I didn't come here to see you," she replied.

"Oh really?" He moved closer to her and Tara hated that she had nowhere to run. No, what she really hated was that running was always her first option.

Running, hiding, staying on the outskirts of life and looking in were Melanie's thing, but Tara had vowed to be different. She had committed, or at least she was trying to commit, and yet...

"You never told me your name," he whispered as his hand reached around to cup the back of her neck, forcing her to tilt back a little so she could look up into his eyes.

Her body trembled. "I don't know..."

Her words were stalled when he leaned in, clearly prepared to kiss her again. As much as Tara wanted that kiss and possibly much more, she knew she had to be careful. They were no longer within the walls of The Corporation, which meant the rules were very different. The code of ethics she'd been told each member swore to uphold had no standing outside of the club. He could do whatever he wanted to her in this elevator, and what she thought he wanted to do was more than she'd bargained for. Something, somewhere in the recesses of her mind continued to warn her. From him? From this place?

The elevator door opened and Tara pushed past him before he had a moment to react. She didn't run, but walked very quickly through the glass doors of the building. She was just about to step into the street to cross over to where the cab she'd paid to wait for her was parked. Then he called to her.

"You never told me your name in New York, but I won't let you slip away this time. I promise you that."

Although she'd stopped moving as soon as he spoke, Tara didn't turn back, couldn't chance looking at him again and feeling that instant pull. Coming here had definitely been a mistake. She wasn't ready for this, was not prepared to become someone else, no matter what her circumstances.

CHAPTER THREE

"Freeze of I'll blow your fuckin' head off," Russ said in a voice that was as lethal, if not more so, than the big black gun he had pointing at her face.

Tara dropped her purse, moving so quickly her back slammed painfully against the door she'd just opened. She cursed. "Is this how you treat all your WITSEC clients?" she asked, rebounding from the brawny six-foot-plus tall man shoving a gun into her face.

She bent down to pick up her purse and heard him swear as he slammed the door behind her. She was walking away as she heard him putting the locks into place.

"I called for backup when I realized you weren't here. There are marshals all over the city looking for you. Don't walk away from me goddammit!" he yelled.

Tara paused just as she was about to take the first step. "Don't you yell at me!" she shouted back, looking coldly into his dark, stormy eyes. "You're not supposed to even be here. I've done my civic duty and you moved on to your next case."

Acting as if she hadn't said a word, Russ continued with his own tirade, his deep, gruff voice vibrating off the walls of the small cottage. "You're fucking irresponsible!"

"Tell me something I don't know," she quipped, then sighed heavily. Tonight had not gone the way she'd planned, and on the cab ride home she'd decided that she shouldn't have planned it in the first place. She shouldn't have ever left this house. But that didn't mean she was going to let the scowling guard get away with yelling at her, especially since he had no business being here. "Are you breaking into my house now? Is that what the government does after I give up my life so they could get a federal conviction?"

She hadn't meant to say it like that, hadn't meant to sound ungrateful for all that they'd done on her behalf, but Russ was such an asshole, and now that she knew he was officially off her case, she wasn't adverse to letting him know it. Still, she was just about to say something else, to try and regain her composure when another man entered the conversation—uninvited, of course.

"There's been a new development," Emilio said.

Tara turned from where she'd been standing near the bay window, that now had the curtains and blinds closed tightly. She'd opened them just this morning to let in the sunlight.

At the top of the stairs was Emilio Alvarez, the marshal that had not only saved her life but had been nice to her when his co-workers had chosen to take the more reserved stance with their witness. His hands were on his hips, dropping to his side as he took the stairs one by one, his booted feet silent on the carpet.

He wore dark cargo pants and a navy blue t-shirt that made his eyes seem brighter, his hair darker. If not for the fact that he was frowning, she would dare to say he was handsome. Tara had thought this before during the days she'd spent with Emilio, that he had kind eyes that seemed to conflict with his warrior's build and grim outlook on life.

Her temples throbbed as she became overwhelmed
with the events of the evening. She'd just run from one
man and now had two of them not only in her house,
but also determined to get in her face. Served her right,
she thought, taking a steadying breath. She should have
listened to her inner voice, the one that sounded way
too much like her mother.

"What are you talking about a new development? I
testified. He was convicted. You packed up and left.
Why are you back?" she asked, not really sure she
wanted the answer, but knowing it was necessary.

"You don't call the shots," Russ added with a
harrumph behind her.

She whirled on him faster than she thought possible
since she felt absolutely exhausted. "This is my house! I
damn well do call the shots here! Now, you tell me
what's going on?" was her question to Emilio who now
stood right beside her.

He was agitated, she could tell because his lips were
in a thin line, the tips of his earlobes red like that apple
sitting amongst an array of fruit in the crystal bowl in
the center of her kitchen island.

She'd only seen Emilio look this way once or twice
before, and each time it had been because of something
the Marshal's Office wouldn't agree to. Tara had
attempted to stay out of the paperwork and policy that
was required to house her safely. In fact, tonight, she'd
been trying like hell not to think about how she'd come
to be here in the first place, instead focusing on the
possibility of a future which, she now figured looked
pretty bleak.

"This is very serious, Tara," Emilio continued.

His voice always lowered whenever he said her
name. It was weird, but not to the point where she
questioned it. It was just something she'd noticed,

especially since in the last months there hadn't been much else going on.

His voice now sounded just as it had that day he'd come to her house in Dalton, the day he'd told her that life would change from that moment on.

"What is it?" she asked, moving to the temporary love seat Emilio had given her as a housewarming gift. Tara sat down heavily, setting her purse on the table. "What's happened?"

"Now you want to know," Russ muttered.

He was standing near the front door as if he really thought she would actually try to make a run for it. Newsflash, her outing hadn't gone as well as she'd anticipated, so she wasn't really looking forward to going back out anytime soon.

"I'll take it from here, Russ," Emilio told the other marshal.

Russ did not like that. Tara knew his pissed off look too well because he wore it all the time. Since the second month that she'd been living in Seal Beach, the first rainy day that he'd come into the small bungalow they'd housed her in, the tall man shaped like a steroid-pumped wrestler had been angry. His thick eyebrows were always furrowed, the strong line of his jaw always ticked with an impatient muscle, his nostrils flaring whenever he looked at her. His skin was like polished bronze and was always shiny, as if it were stretched to capacity over his bulging muscles. The bald head only completed his look of intimidation. She turned away from him quickly.

"Right," she heard Russ muttering as he left them alone. A few moments later the front door slammed.

"He's pretty pissed that you were able to sneak out without him knowing," Emilio said, a soft smile ghosting his lips as he sat across from her.

It was a fake smile. She'd seen those on him before. He liked to try and humor her, and because she never complained about it, he continued, believing that it was actually working. Truth be told, it wasn't because she didn't really care about humor or laughter or any of those other frivolous emotions anymore. She had no family, no real identity and, in her mind, no purpose. While that sounded pretty damned dismal and a bit pathetic, it was her simple truth.

"How was I sneaking out when I didn't know I was still on lockdown or being watched?" she snapped back.

Emilio stared at her for a second before speaking. Absently, she thought the thick brows and mustache worked for his olive complexion. It made him appear serious, lethal, both of which she figured he needed to perform his job.

"Around 10:30 a black sedan rode down the block," he told her. "At 10:45, it passed the house again. Same sedan, same tags that Russ ran the first trip around and came up with some corporate title that we're researching now."

A few simple sentences spoken in less than a minute that sent tiny spikes of fear marching down Tara's spine. She sat up straighter in the chair, watching Emilio talk with much more interest now.

"At 11:15, the sedan parked at the corner. Russ got out of his truck and walked up to your door. He used the key to get in and disengaged the alarm system. Your dog, who I've realized over the past months acts as your personal alarm system, began barking. Seconds later Russ discovered you were already gone. He called for backup and immediately went outside to approach the sedan."

He paused there, for effect she figured. It was unnecessary. She was already terrified at the implications.

"It was gone."

Tara flattened her palms on her knees, not sure what else she should do to keep them from shaking.

She let out the breath she hadn't known she'd been holding and looked out the window. This side of the house offered a partial view of the beach and a good portion of her yard since she was an end unit. At this moment all she saw was darkness, and it frightened her more.

"I left at ten o'clock, and I didn't see any sedan," she told him, as if that really mattered now.

"Why did you leave?" he asked simply.

"How do the others stay?" she asked instead, turning to look at him once more. "How do the other people you've relocated manage to stay trapped in their house until the trial and sometimes even afterwards? How do they find this new life you're so graciously giving them and does it always work out or do they crack from the pressure?"

"You get to continue living," Emilio told her. "That's all that matters, Tara, is that you are alive, period."

She shook her head, even though she knew there was some truth to what he was saying. "It's not living if I don't have any family or any friends. I'm just existing."

"Is that what you were looking for tonight? A friend? Or a family member? Which one did you think you were going to find, or was the reason you left more rooted in what you could see out there that you couldn't in here?"

She hated that he knew everything about her. Hated, and sort of wondered about that fact on an almost daily basis. The morning after Emilio had taken her from her home in Dalton, he'd poured both of them a cup of coffee in the outdated kitchen in that first WITSEC house and sat across from her just like he was now, talking to her about everything from her mother's suicide three years ago to the incident at her school that had almost cost her the job of her dreams, and finally to how she'd witnessed Jana's death.

Every answer to every question had been given honestly and out of fear. There was no way around it, she'd figured. But now, she'd wished there had been a way to keep her secret. Because that secret was why he was looking at her now as if he could barely stomach her presence. He didn't look at her this way often, but every now and then she'd catch him staring and she knew he was wondering about her sexual preference, about the hobby she'd preferred over real human interaction.

"I didn't see anything," she said quietly, hoping he couldn't hear the disappointment that laced her tone.

"But you wanted to, you were looking for something to see?"

He was pushing her, but Tara didn't know which way he was expecting her to go. She figured, once more, that the truth was probably the best. At least part of the truth.

"Yes. I need...I mean, I wanted to see something. But I didn't."

"Why?"

"Because I can't see from here!" she yelled, startling herself at the emotionally charged outburst. "You fixed it so that there's nothing for me to see from the comfort of my own home. That worked during the trial, but am I supposed to keep those restrictions for the rest of my life?"

Tara was sad that she was no longer a high school guidance counselor helping to set new adults on the right path in life. She was depressed about having no family and no friends to turn to, and wondered whether those circumstances were dictated by this current situation or a divine authority.

Tonight's events had sent her into a spiral of despair, when in reality, there was much she should be thankful for. She was alive, and in the last few months had managed to build quite a successful business. Her bank account now was even bigger than it had been before Jana's murder, hence the ability to purchase her own home—even though Russ had really hated that idea. But Emilio had agreed that she needed to feel like this life was really hers.

She desperately wanted to feel that way, she did. Yet once again, what she wanted for herself and what the world dropped in her lap were two totally different things.

"We've restricted your internet access because Penelli and his crew are smarter than most people give them credit for. The moment you made that 911 call and reported that murder, they knew who and what you were. That's why we had to get you out of there so quickly. Do you think they're not monitoring the porn sites for anyone that remotely sounds like you?"

"It's not porn," she said so quietly she hadn't thought he'd heard her. But he had, the audible outtake of breath told her that. "Not to me."

"But you're not that person anymore, Tara. You're a very attractive woman who can just as easily go out and find a man to give you whatever you could imagine just to see you smile. You don't have to stand on the outside looking at others. It's just not necessary."

He had no idea how necessary it was, especially for her.

"None of this should matter anymore. I did what you needed me to do. I sat in the courtroom for three days answering every question they threw at me. You packed up and left my house. You said it was finally over," she paused, taking a deep breath and releasing it slowly. "Do you think they know I'm here? Were they coming to kill me tonight?"

Emilio leaned forward, his elbows resting on his knees as he stared at her. On his right arm was a black wristwatch that Tara suspected was more than just a watch. There were no rings on his fingers and no earrings in his ears, even though the left one was clearly pierced. He watched her seriously, trying to decide if he should sugarcoat the truth or just serve it strong and hot the way she liked her coffee.

"The truth usually comes faster," she said, giving him a half-smile.

He nodded. "Yes. I think they were coming to kill you."

At his parents' palatial estate in Brentwood, Jack sat in a lounge chair on the veranda, nursing the same glass of wine he'd had at dinner. The sun was just setting, casting a glittering glow over the surface of the infinity pool just 15 feet from where he was lounging.

His brother, Jerald, had come out with him, but Jack hadn't bothered to see where he sat. The clicking of heels on the Italian tiled floor signaled his mother's entrance, and that meant his father would follow shortly behind. This house sat on five acres of land, rising to the top of a small hill like a giant looking down into the valley and the townspeople below. Only there weren't any townspeople, just lush green grass, two guesthouses and his mother's expansive gardens. When they'd purchased this house 10 years ago, Jack had been the first one to say they didn't need all this space. Jason had backed him up, trying to convince Lydia, who they all knew favored her youngest son, that they should look into a condo instead. Jerald, who was the mediator— he'd been defaulted to that status by the order of his birth—had lobbied that they could use the house for business functions so it would also serve as a huge investment for Carrington Enterprises, a thought which hadn't crossed Jeffrey Carrington's mind, but was a fabulous notion nonetheless.

They'd entertained only mildly before Jeffrey had retired, but since that day a year and a half ago, there had been more parties and brunches here than Jack could count. Most of them he'd found some reason not to attend. One excuse was just as good as another as long as he could keep his distance. It hadn't always been that way where his family was concerned and Jack wondered when the change had occurred. When had he started to feel like being in the same room with them was the biggest lie of all?

Probably around the time he decided that a long-term relationship, marriage and children, was definitely not for him. How could he ask a wife to be all he needed, all he desired her to be, when those things might not seem normal? And how could he explain his compulsion to be at the club with likeminded individuals? And why should he have to?

More accurately, however, the change in how he felt when around his family had come just after he'd first seen her at the club in New York, he thought with startling clarity.

"How about you, Jack?"

The hand slapping on his right shoulder was what alerted Jack to the fact that they were speaking to him. Otherwise his mind had been taking him to another place, another revelation that had his heart beating just a little faster.

"What?" was Jack's reply as he readjusted himself in the chair, bringing his wine to his lips to take a sip. His mouth had suddenly gone dry.

"Mom was asking about grandchildren," Jerald said, a sly grin spreading across his face. "I told her I didn't have a definite ETA on any for her. So what about you?"

He could have choked on his wine, spitting the dark liquid all over his tan slacks and white polo shirt. But Jack never showed his hand, nor any weakness that he might possess. So what if his fingers tightened around the base of his glass as he lowered his arm slowly, his gaze on his younger brother even. He would not lose his cool the way he suspected Jerald wanted him to.

"I happen to have a definite ETA," Jack replied, bringing on arched brows from his mother and an interested glance from his father.

Lydia had taken the lounge chair across from Jack while Jeffrey sat at the end of his wife's chair, glass of brandy in hand. Looking at them, Jack realized how much he really did love and respect them, not only as his parents, but as a couple. They'd had some rocky times. He knew this because he was older and he'd heard the early morning arguments that were usually followed with a cordial silence throughout the rest of the day. His father had worked much harder than his mother had thought was necessary since they both had money of their own outside of Carrington Enterprises. But Jeffrey had wanted to build his own fortune, to stand on his own two feet, he'd often told Jack. And so he'd spent endless nights away from home, away from his family, and Lydia hadn't responded well to that. In the end they always rebounded though, always ended up hugging and kissing when they didn't think any of the boys were watching. They were deeply in love. Jack could see that even now as his father absently rubbed his mother's leg and his mother's hand instantly came down to cover her husband's. They were connected, joined by some emotional bond that Jack knew he'd never experience.

"Marriage and kids aren't in the cards for me," he said bluntly.

"You planning on living a life of celibacy?" was Jeffrey's quick question, followed by his gruff laughter.

"That'll be the day," Jerald chimed in.

Jerald was dressed casually, as was his norm. He was a financial investor by day, during which time he said he had to choke on too tight ties and felt stifled by dress shirts and pants. So when his work day was over, he quickly shifted to relaxed mode. He was probably the only one of the Carrington men that could make that transition so quickly. He was also a wiseass.

"It's just not for me," Jack continued, knowing that still wasn't going to be enough, especially not since his mother had sat up completely and was now narrowing her hazel eyes at him.

"How do you know it's not for you if you've never given it a try?" she asked earnestly.

He resisted the urge to shrug and instead stood, emptying his glass of wine—finally—and walking over until he stood behind the bar they had outside.

"Look, Jason and Celise are married now. The resort's expanding, Celise's restaurant is expanding. They're bound to start spitting out kids any minute now," he talked while fixing himself another drink. Something a little stronger this time—vodka.

"And you're an eligible bachelor with a good head on your shoulders, a financially secure future, and you don't look half bad," Lydia continued. "There's no reason you can't find the same happiness that your brother has."

Jack downed half the vodka, loving the sting at the back of his throat and the warmth spreading slowly into his gut. "There's one really good reason," he told her. "I don't want to."

"I hear Soleil's back in town," Jerald added, plopping down into the chair that Jack had vacated.

"Good," Jack quipped. "You should give her a call. She's into sharing and all that."

Soleil Ducovney was the only child of Winston Ducovney, probably the best and certainly the wealthiest jeweler in the United States. She was Jason's age, which made her five years younger than Jack. During her freshman year of college she'd snuck into Jason's room and slipped into his bed naked. Four years later, she'd appeared in the back of a limousine Jack was riding in more than eager to show him all she'd learned in the years since he'd seen her. And because being rebuffed by one Carrington wasn't enough, Jerald had found her naked in his pool one evening when he'd returned from work. Jack might be inclined to call her a slut, but none of the brothers had ever been horny enough to actually sleep with her. In fact, they'd never even considered dating her, which had not gone over well with the pampered princess. Jack couldn't even remember how long she'd been abroad, and learning that she had recently returned to Beverly Hills was of absolutely no significance to him.

"Look, there are people who are made for the grand institute of marriage, the commitment and the sacrifice. Those people make it work no matter what. Their love sees them through, they would say. Procreating is a likeminded goal they share and work at with vigor. Their family is built, their home safe and secure and their life proceeds, until it ends," he said, pausing to take another gulp of his drink.

"Wow, Jack, that's pretty cynical don't you think?" Jerald asked with a frown.

"Really, son, you must—"

Jack held up a hand to halt his mother's next words.

"I wasn't finished," he told the three that were staring at him as if he must have another head growing out of his neck to have spoken so blandly against getting married and starting a family. "I used to think about doing all those things, finding the woman, falling in love, marrying her, having kids, all that good stuff wrapped neatly in a bow. Then I grew up. Marriage is not for everyone and if more people would come to terms with that before walking down the aisle, the divorce rate wouldn't be as high as it is now. I'm one of the few that can accept this is not for me. I like my life exactly as it is and do not plan on changing it."

His words came out like some type of solemn vow. Jack tried not to frown at that, or at the pretty milk chocolate complexion and pert little mouth of a woman whose name he'd learned from looking at the club's restricted guest list.

"That was an eloquent speech, Jack my boy," Jeffrey said, coming to a stand. He leaned over to kiss his wife's forehead when she opened her mouth to speak again. The action silenced Lydia, which to Jack was a surprise. His mother was not a woman easily silenced. "You just keep on working and keep on living the way you do, if that's what makes you happy."

"Thanks, Dad," Jack said deciding not to take this conversation any further if he didn't absolutely have to.

"Don't thank me. I want to stop talking about this marriage and grandkids thing so I can ask how that RGA merger is coming along. I hear there's some resistance."

Jack smiled at his father and happily answered his question, feeling a lightness in his steps as he finally left his parents' house 45 minutes later. He wasn't getting married or having kids and his family finally understood his reasons why, he thought as he'd slipped behind the wheel of his black amethyst Jaguar F-Type Coupe.

Hours later when Jack lay in his king-sized bed, in the master suite of his three-bedroom condo in Granite Park Place, staring up at the ceiling, he thought of a woman who had captured his attention more completely than any other. When he'd attempted to sleep, closing his eyes in the darkened room, he saw her in that hot pink dress that clung to every silken curve of her body. He saw her brown eyes, long curling lashes and high cheekbones, her pert mouth and…his gaze rested there.

That night in New York, more than a year ago now, she'd been wearing black, a skirt that hugged her tight ass and a halter top that cupped her high breasts. The bare skin of her torso had caught his attention then, along with the smooth, milk chocolate complexion and the tiny flirty turquoise ball that dangled from her belly button. She'd been flirty and friendly, more than willing to fall into his arms, into the kiss that she'd instigated.

Jack had been simply watching the comings and goings of members and guests. The New York club had a trendy hip décor with its black painted walls and white tiled floors. The chair he was seated in wasn't as comfortable as he'd like. Its high hard back was leather, but there were no arms. Still, he'd found the place in the corner discreet enough, that he could unwind from 12 hours of meetings and the still incomplete acquisition.

She'd come in alone, smiling and greeting people as if she knew everyone there by name. Jack had watched her from the moment she stepped into the room until the second she stood in front of him, hands on her hips, breasts rising and falling with her steady breath.

"Can I sit down?" she asked daringly, one perfectly curved brow arching.

He'd nodded, not sure yet how this would play out but certain he wanted to test the waters. She was young and eager, he'd surmised that already. She was in the club, which meant either she knew someone who had firsthand knowledge of what went on here or that she'd found out about the place and made it a point to get to know somebody who knew what went on here. Did this mean she was up for the sessions Jack preferred? He wasn't sure, but he was going to soon find out.

When he'd thought she would turn her back to him and sit on his lap, rubbing her cute little ass against his steadily hardening dick, teasing him in a fashion he guessed she was good at, she didn't. Instead she stepped forward, lifting one leg slightly so she could straddle him. She'd giggled as she scooted closer to him, the warmth from between her legs settling over the zipper of his pants. She'd placed her palms on his shoulders and leaned into him, whispering into his ear, "Is anyone watching?"

Jack had to lean over slightly to put his glass on the floor. When he was facing her once more, he looked over her shoulder to see three other men in the room, two of them gazing in their direction, very interested in what was going to happen next.

"Yes," he'd replied, and before he could say another word, her lips were on his, her tongue diving deep into his mouth.

He'd cupped her ass, loving the hunger all but vibrating throughout her entire body, the energy sizzling through the air around. She obviously wanted someone, anyone, to see him fuck her, and while Jack was usually the one in charge, the one calling the shots, giving all the direction, he'd followed her lead, getting a certain thrill out of being seen driving deep into this hot little number.

And then he'd stopped. All this time later he still
didn't know why, but he'd pulled his mouth away from
hers, staring directly into her eyes as he said, "Get up."

She'd frowned, but hadn't hesitated to shimmy
herself right off his lap and onto the next, more willing
guy—a tall, dark-haired man dressed in all black
frowning as if he might already know her. For the rest
of the night Jack had made sure she was within his
sights. He'd given up his opportunity to sleep with her,
but felt a tugging towards her that he couldn't quite
explain. After another hour, his phone had vibrated and
he'd looked at the text, relieved and excited that the
CEO had finally come to his senses. The deal was
going through, contracts to be signed first thing in the
morning. He'd decided to leave the club without having
any more satisfaction other than watching the girl in
black. It was then that he realized she was gone.

With a shrug, he'd returned to his hotel and the next
day closed the deal. While he was on the plane back to
L.A. he'd thought about her again, about her brown
eyes and quick smile and soft, pleasing lips. From that
day on, there hadn't been a day that he hadn't seen her
face and remembered the feel of her in his hands. That
time he hadn't thought to ask the hostess on duty who
she was.

He hadn't been foolish enough to make the same
mistake twice. She'd looked at him as if he were some
rapist chasing her down on the street on Friday night.
That had been what made him pause and all but secured
that he would not follow her outside or attempt to
coerce her in anyway.

Jack wasn't in the business of scaring women or
doing anything that gave the impression that he would
hurt them in any way. She—Tara Sullivan—had looked
as if her life depended on getting as far away from him
as fast as she possibly could. She'd been the total

opposite of how she'd acted in New York and he wanted to know why. He wanted to know if there was something he could do to make it better. Something he could say, or buy, or anything.

So as Jack made his way back into his condo tonight, he was not surprised to find himself thinking about her again. She'd been on his mind all day yesterday as he'd worked a few hours at the office and then when he'd come home and attempted to do even more work. Today, as he'd known he was having dinner with his parents, he'd tried to clear his mind, spending the morning at the gym and the afternoon listening to his favorite jazz collection, but it hadn't worked.

Jack's cell phone rang the moment he closed and locked his door behind him. He pulled the mobile free of its clip to answer.

"Ready for my report?"

"Go ahead," Jack instructed, moving into the living room and taking a seat on the couch. He hadn't bothered with the lamps. The blinds to French doors leading out to the deck were open, so the city lights cast the room in a serene glow.

"Tara Sullivan, age 29, 5' 6½", turning 30 next May. Address: 9087B Sunnydale Court, Seal Beach, California. Owner and designer of Vicious Designs, an online graphic design company that's been in business for less than a year but is seeing nothing but profit so far."

"That's it?" Jack asked.

Trent Donovan chuckled. "You want her blood type and the hospital she was born at too?"

Jack didn't find that funny. First thing yesterday morning he'd called Trent, owner of D&D Private Investigations and an old friend. If there was one thing Trent was good at, besides being a Navy SEAL and one of the infamous Triple Threat Donovan brothers, it was finding out every sordid detail in a person's life. Carrington Enterprises had D&D on a monthly retainer for the detailed background checks they performed on each one of the shareholders in every one of the companies they'd been interested in acquiring.

"I know there has to be more than that," he continued. "What did you find about the time she was in New York? Was she living there? Was she married?"

"Nada," Trent told him. "There's nothing before she started the online business. I found that she just purchased a home, but she must have paid in cash since there's only a deed listed in her name, but no bank loan. No previous jobs, nothing accumulated in social security. Nothing. This girl's cleaner than anybody I've ever investigated."

Jack rubbed a finger over his chin. "And that's not good," he said uneasily.

"No," Trent concurred. "That's not good."

CHAPTER FOUR

Tara walked down to the beach glancing upward at the gold streaked sky, watching the sun set for the evening. Up ahead glistening rays shimmered over the water as the waves rose and crashed against the shore. Beside her Vicious yipped and ran in circles until finally Tara stopped, knelt down and unclipped the leash from the dog's collar. Vicious apparently loved sunsets on the beach as much as Tara.

After working the better part of the day on design projects, Tara was more than ready to stretch her legs and get some fresh air. With her sandals dangling from one hand, she scrunched her toes in the warm sand the moment she was on the beach. Inhaling long and slow, exhaling just as deeply, she tried to clear her mind, to relax—something she hadn't been doing lately. After the trial had concluded, she'd thought relaxation would come a little easier. How wrong she'd been. The first couple of weeks had been filled with grief all over again at losing Jana to such a malicious and conniving killer. Then, when she'd thought she'd finally snapped out of that and was ready to begin again, she froze like a kid with her hand caught in the candy jar.

He'd wanted her. Desire had been clear in Jackson Carrington's dark, brooding gaze. It had sizzled along her skin as he stood close to her in that elevator. And even as she'd walked away from him, the electricity between them had seemed to reach right out like tentacles, following her not only to the cab but back to her house where it had quickly been extinguished by her surprise guests.

Now, knowing that she might possibly still be on the Mafia's most wanted list created a knot between her shoulders that pressed down on her like a heavy weight. Tension culminated at the base of her neck and resulted in headaches that sometimes held her captive in bed for hours on end. She had lost weight over the last couple of months because her appetite was little to none.

All this coupled with overwhelming sadness was beginning to take its toll. It had taken her twice the time to complete a book cover design than it had months ago when she first started her company. She knew that to keep up her good reputation, she would have to snap out of this state of depression, and she prayed for any type of solace to get her there. But according to her mother, no god would ever hear her prayers. Because she was a sinner, from her thoughts to the actions she'd almost taken last night, she was tainted. And even though right at this moment she was more sexually repressed than any devout believer she could imagine, Tara couldn't help but consider it true on some level.

As for right now, this walk would have to suffice as the only tension relief she would be afforded. There were few people down at this end of the beach, which was part of the reason she'd selected this house. It was secluded enough that she'd thought she would never have to worry about being found. Apparently, she'd been wrong. Out of the corner of her eye to the right she saw Russ, his hulking form clumsily moving over the rocks, hating the trek in the sand she insisted on taking.

Emilio had explained that he would research the ownership of that black sedan Russ had seen outside of her house a few days ago. When she'd inquired if she would be going back to 24 hour marshal service again, he'd told her no. Officially, they'd completed their assignment where she was concerned. Just as she'd thought she'd finished hers. But if there was a new threat...she didn't want to think about that. Yet apparently, Russ did.

She decided to ignore him. It was best that way because she really didn't feel like getting into a verbal altercation with the man and his prickly personality. If he wanted to watch her taking a walk with Vicious, then he certainly could. In fact, a part of her felt better that he was, but she'd never tell him that.

Vicious' incessant barking grabbed her attention and Tara looked up to see her pretty white dog covered in sand, dripping wet. She'd gone into the water again. Tara giggled, running to the puppy and falling to her knees in the sand to pick her up. It was when she'd lifted Vicious, snuggled her to her chin, laughing more as she tried to admonish the hyper dog, that she saw someone approaching.

It was a man that had her heart pounding just a little faster in her chest. A man she thought she'd never see again. Jackson Carrington.

Immediately Tara came to her feet, Vicious in hand as she stood perfectly still, wondering what would happen next. Abruptly she realized that's how she'd been living each day since the marshals showed up at her house, contemplating just when the other proverbial shoe would drop. It was a sad way to live, she admitted to herself just as the man came to a stop in front of her.

"Hello," he spoke, looking down at her, those dark, hypnotic eyes watching her with the same intensity he had at the club.

"What are you doing here?" she asked before she could stop herself. "I mean, hello." She licked her now dry lips, adjusting her hold on Vicious as the dog was anxious to get down and run some more.

He had thick eyebrows, she noticed as Jack's brow furrowed. They weren't messy or bushy, just thick. The kind a woman would kill for.

"I wanted to see you again," he replied in a tone that was purely unapologetic. "Are you feeling better today?"

"What? Oh, the other night, yes, I'm fine. Thank you for asking." And now you go about your business, she thought as a breeze tossed wayward strands of her hair into her face. She attempted to turn her head, hoping that would blow them in the other direction, but it didn't work.

Before she could decide whether to put down her dog and fix her hair or to simply stand there staring at him through the annoying strands, his hand was coming towards her face. Fingers that didn't look like they should have a gentle touch pushed the hair away slowly, tucking it back behind her ear. Those same fingers brushed lightly over the sensitive skin beneath her ear and down her neck, and Tara shivered. He obviously did not notice her reaction because in the next second, he was repeating the motion, laying hair behind the other ear, touching her neck once more.

She watched his movements, felt slightly mesmerized by the corded muscles in the lower half of his arm, the strength his wide hands exuded. No other part of his body moved, just as it hadn't that night at the club. He was a very restrained man; whatever movements he made were purposeful, controlled. The thought made her mouth water and her heart hammer wildly in her chest.

"Thanks," she whispered, looking away from him and down at Vicious, who obediently turned to lick her chin.

"If you're feeling better, I'd like to take you to dinner. I can wait for you to put your dog inside," he told her as if he knew her answer would be yes.

And really, why shouldn't it be? He was Jackson Carrington after all. The morning after seeing him at the club she'd Googled him and found more than enough information about the handsome, if not a bit reclusive, millionaire, who could possibly own half the corporations in the U.S. if he weren't so busy selling them off piece by piece. He was 36 years old, the eldest of three boys born into a family of wealth and prestige. In other words, he had absolutely no business standing on Seal Beach with Tara—the woman with no real identity and a fetish that may or may not have sealed her fate in hell—and inviting her to dinner.

"I don't think so," she replied hurriedly, shaking her head. "I've got a lot of work to get to."

She said that because it sounded better than, "I'm a train wreck and you shouldn't waste your time with me." At least in her mind it did.

Again, there was that effortless control. His facial expression did not change, almost as if she hadn't spoken at all. "Then we'll go tomorrow night. I'll pick you up at seven."

"No, I—"

Her words were cut off as this time those long, piano fingers were touching her lips, effectively halting the rest of her objection.

"Are you seeing someone else?" he asked.

She shook her head.

"Will you be in the hospital or some other way incapacitated and unable to eat?"

Again her head was shaking, his fingers still touching her lips.

"Then I will be here at seven."

He let his hand move slowly from her lips to pet Vicious, who barked but did not snap at him as she did the marshals.

"Cute dog," he said looking back to her, his brows no longer furrowed. Yet his face still held a serious gaze. "I'll see you tomorrow."

She was about to nod, and then thought better of the whole mute persona and cleared her throat before replying, "Okay. But it will just be dinner."

When he only continued to stare and then finally said, "Have a goodnight, Tara," she thought he might actually have only one facial expression.

"Wait," she yelled to him after he'd turned and taken a couple of steps away from her. "How did you know my name and where I live?"

He turned back to her then, the fading sun capturing him in a golden hue so that he looked almost ethereal standing there in his linen pants and button-front shirt.

"When something interests me, I make it my business to know all there is to know about it. Or in this case, about you."

Tara didn't respond again but let him walk away because her next words were going to be somewhere along the lines of "Oh no, you don't really want to know everything about me."

After standing there a few minutes more, until Jackson had turned up the path to the dock and disappeared from her sight, Tara turned to go back home.

She gasped as Russ had left his perch a couple feet back and now stood right in her face. Vicious barked and was able to bound right out of her startled master's arms. But she didn't leave Tara. Instead the bichon frisé stood right beside Russ, growling as if she were a pit bull.

"Dammit!" Tara yelled, taking a step back and pressing a hand to her rapidly beating heart. "You scared the crap out of me."

Russ scowled down at her. "I scared you, but you had no problem letting some guy you don't even know walk up to you and touch you intimately on a private beach. All while knowing someone is out to kill you."

"Emilio said you're not sure who owns that sedan or if they were really looking for me," she replied in defense, even though that wasn't quite what Emilio had told her. "Besides, I have a right to a life! I have a right to meet new people and to move on. I did what I was supposed to do!" she yelled.

"And now I'm doing the same," he told her as he reached out to grab her by the arm.

"Let me go you big idiot! I know my way home."

His lips actually peeled back from his teeth as he continued to glare angrily at her. But a second or so later, he did release his grip, pulling his hand back as if by touching her he may have contracted some deadly disease. Tara refused to feel offended. If he thought he could catch something by touching her, good. Maybe he'd keep his damned hands off from now on.

"Until Emilio comes back with an official report saying there's a true threat, I'd appreciate it if you kept your distance," she told him before walking around his hulking form and heading up to her house, not bothering to wait for a reply.

CHAPTER FIVE

She smelled like heaven.

Of course he'd never been there, but Jack was positive the soft, alluring fragrance that emanated from her skin, drifting up through his nostrils as he'd leaned in to kiss her cheek when she opened the door, was the closest comparison to absolute perfection.

The fact that she'd taken a hurried step back just as his lips had brushed her smooth skin alerted him once more to the fact that there was more to this woman than met the eye. It was that "more" that made it impossible to keep thoughts of her from his mind. He'd felt like a kid at Christmas sitting behind his desk attempting to concentrate, yet actually counting the hours until he could see her.

Finally, at 3:30 he'd given up the pretense, packed the contracts that he had been unable to focus on today into his briefcase and left the building. He'd driven himself home and taken a long shower, hoping to rinse some of the salacious thoughts he'd been having about Tara from his mind. It hadn't worked.

His dick had been rock hard the moment he stripped off his clothes, from thinking about her long legs wrapped around him as she rode him while he was driving his car. Once the water slapped against his skin, Jack prayed the sting of its heated temperature would be enough to snap him out of the aroused trance. He'd been wrong. The warm trickle of water only served to stimulate him even more, until he had to grit his teeth to keep from grabbing his length and finding his own pleasure.

For Jack that had never been an option. He wanted his pleasure at the hands of another. To be precise he wanted his pleasure between the soft curve of her lips, against the heated pad of her tongue. He wanted this woman with a need so urgent, so predominant, he had to gulp at its potency.

He was not a man easily shaken. Years of sitting across board room tables from billionaires desperate to hold on to their fortunes had given him a stellar poker face that matched his serious demeanor completely. At that moment Jack had the power to either make those dreams come true or be the boot to trample over them. Most times he did the trampling. Carrington Enterprises' reputation dictated no other option. His father had taught him to take no prisoners in business transactions and to do whatever was necessary to reap the rewards for Carrington. In his personal life, he was guilty of doing the same, helping to create a club that would cater to every pleasurable desire so that this dating process would be obsolete.

Jack didn't date. He didn't oblige traditional courtships, nor did he subscribe to where dating would ultimately lead. His personality, his birthright and his upbringing all dictated that he be a leader in all things, that if he wanted something, he would have it.

Yet, as he stepped out of the shower, feet touching the cool marble tiles, water dripping from his naked body, there was an eerie feeling in his gut where she was concerned. He wanted her in a way he could never recall wanting anything and prayed that desire would not weaken him. Methodically he moved through the motions of getting dressed. Foregoing a fresh shave he smoothed the thin layer of hair on his face down with his palms. After a pass with the towel, he slipped into boxer briefs and undershirt before the white dress shirt, black pants and vest. Shoes, watch, cologne, and he was ready and not a moment too soon, because with each familiar motion he'd thought of what Tara would be wearing tonight.

Would her hair be pulled back neatly in that conservative bun that made his fingers itch to pull it free? Or would it be in a messy ponytail as he'd seen it yesterday, with sexy little strands blowing in her face, scraping against the smooth skin of her cheek? Would her dress be formfitting and enticing as it had been at the club a few nights ago, or loose and flowing as the skirt she wore yesterday? His body tightened with the thoughts as he snatched the keys from the marble and glass table by his front door and headed out.

It wasn't often that Jack used a driver, unlike his father who never left home without Claude, who had been in the Carrington's employ for more than twenty years now. Tonight, however, Jack knew he didn't want to miss one moment of being close to Tara. So he'd reserved a chauffeur, instructing the service that the driver use the platinum Phantom that Jack kept parked in his secure area of the building's parking garage.

Jack stepped off the private elevator that took him down to the lower level of the building. Mercer, who was Jack's preferred driver from the only car service in town that the executive used, was standing by the back passenger side door of the Phantom. With a nod Jack greeted the tall, thin man and slipped onto the back leather seats, settling in for the ride to Seal Beach.

Tara's heart lurched as the car slowed, coming to a complete stop directly in front of her door.

She instantly thought about the sedan that Russ had seen parked at the corner of her block just days prior. But this was no sedan. It was a Rolls-Royce, a beautiful shiny one that gave her just another reason to pause.

She'd agreed to this date with Jackson for two reasons: One, because she knew Russ was near and the longer she stood on the beach talking to Jack, the more likely it was that the overzealous marshal would interrupt; and, two, because the voice in her head, the one that was taking complete hold of the new-identity, new-life mantra, had screamed for her to say "yes."

With the decision made, she'd thrown herself into her work all day long. Surprisingly, she managed to get more done today than she had in the weeks since the trial. She'd listened to music, some contemporary station that played songs she knew the lyrics to, and on more than one occasion caught herself singing along. Overall, she'd felt lighter and more at ease today than she had in the last year. Until this very moment.

From her position standing just to the side of the bay windows in her living room, she peaked through the blinds to see a man dressed in a black suit climb out of the driver's side and go to the back to open the door. Her mouth actually went dry as she watched Jackson step out of the car.

He was well over six feet tall, she figured since she'd had to crane her neck to see him while standing on the beach yesterday. Sometimes taller men didn't pull off dress clothes well. Of course, she figured that may have been because those clothes weren't expertly tailored and expensive as she suspected Jackson's were. He was gorgeous as his long stride covered the walkway leading to her house. The slacks and vest were a nice, modern look that outlined his toned physique perfectly. Her gaze rested on his muscled thighs as he moved to the spot where she imagined the length of his rigid erection would rest.

And while that had her breaths coming quicker, it was the butter tone of his skin, shadowed by the light sprinkle of beard and mustache that had her breath catching. She'd noticed yesterday a deep dimple in his chin that peeked just beneath the hair and the medium thickness of his lips. Actually, she'd noticed how handsome he was at the club. His piercing gaze made her mouth water, her nipples pucker and her center...well, she was just not going to go there. Not tonight and not any night.

This was just dinner and she was only going because she suspected that Jackson Carrington was not a man used to being denied. Saying no to this dinner would probably only have prompted him to ask again and again, until she'd finally given in. So she'd cut her loses and hopefully avoided a very uncomfortable exchange between them.

The brisk knock on the door startled her and she jumped away from the window as if she'd been caught watching. Again.

Clearing her throat and ordering her heart to return to its normal rhythm, Tara walked slowly to the door, her four inch heels moving quietly over the carpeted floor.

"Hello," she said after opening the door.

He didn't instantly reply, but took a step towards her instead. Tara backed up, not really expecting him to come inside. His arm was immediately going around her waist then, holding her still.

"Hello," he replied, his voice deep, thick, arousing.

It seemed like a blissful eternity they stood that way, her arms at her sides, his one wrapped around her, her breasts pressing against his torso, and Vicious barking happily as she ran circles around them.

"Ah, I need to get my purse," Tara said when the heat flowing like a raging river throughout her body threatened to make her sweat. She said the words and thought she should be moving with them, but remained perfectly still.

He didn't budge. "I'll take care of everything you need."

The words sounded earnest and final at the same time. She blinked and forced herself to move this time. "We should go," she told him this time, pressing her palms to his chest and attempting to push away.

"We should," he repeated, a frown marring his brow, before he released her.

She almost breathed a sigh of relief, but kept it in as she hurriedly moved to the chair where she'd tossed her bolero jacket and purse.

"It's warm. You won't need the jacket," he said from behind her.

"Sometimes the air conditioning in restaurants is up too high, so I like to be on the safe side," she was saying while shooing Vicious into the kitchen and turning back to him. "I'm ready to go now."

Tara was ready for something more, she thought alarmingly. Her entire body tingled with awareness and a small part of her wanted to run upstairs and lock herself in her bedroom. But that was out of the question. There would be no running away tonight. She'd already decided that while she showered. She'd agreed to the date and she was going to see it through. She owed herself that much.

After she'd checked the alarm system and the locks, he touched a hand to her elbow, guiding her down the walkway to where the car door was waiting open for her. Instinctively, and with just a touch of contemplation, Tara looked around to see if the marshal's truck was parked anywhere on her street.

Even though her case was over it seemed they, especially Russ, was always still lurking around. When she saw no one and no vehicle, she continued to move easily into the vehicle, sliding all the way to the window on the opposite side.

"You don't have to run from me, Tara," he said after a few moments of traveling in silence. "It's not my intention to hurt you."

For a brief second, Tara wondered why he'd said those specific words. Could he perchance know about her past, about the possibility that someone might be out to kill her? Could he be the one in the sedan, or had he sent the sedan to watch her house? Her mind was alight with questions that the calmer, more focused part of her eventually pushed aside. *Deal with the here and now, live in this moment.* Jana used to say that to her.

"I'm not running, Jackson," she said more to herself than him, at the same time loving the way his name felt on her lips. It had been the first time she'd said it aloud and it made her turn immediately to look at him.

His side profile was just as satisfying as the front, if not a little more so, since it gave her a closer view of his muscled arms and thighs pressing against the material of his clothes. He smelled good too, like something rich and smooth.

"Good. I don't like to chase," he told her, reaching out a hand and once again touching her waist.

With not much effort he was able to slide her across the seat until the sides of their bodies were touching, instantly sending the temperature in the back of the car soaring. He kept that arm around her waist and leaned in closer to whisper into her ear.

"But, make no mistake, Tara Sullivan, I would chase you. All the way to the ends of the earth, is how far I'd go to have you."

She wanted to say something witty, but also blasé, to act as if his words, the feel of his warm breath against her skin, the close proximity...that none of that had affected her. But it would be a lie and for tonight she'd sworn she wouldn't lie to herself about what she was feeling or how she wanted to act.

Live in the moment.

The words replayed in her mind, had her turning her head so that now they were nose to nose. And this time she kissed him.

Without another thought one of her hands was going behind his head, pulling his mouth down on hers. He reacted instantly, pressing his tongue against her lips until she opened her mouth to him. It was like 4th of July fireworks sparkling and detonating inside her mind as the warmth of his tongue tangled around hers.

In the next instant and with the help of the hand he'd already had around her waist, Tara felt herself being lifted from the seat and plopped down onto Jackson's lap, directly over his already aroused dick. Every nerve in her body reacted and at once she pressed her center into him, her breasts smashing against his chest as he kissed her fervently. His hands were strong, cupping her ass, holding her in place over his erection while his mouth expertly worked hers into a frenzy.

She couldn't breathe, air lodging in her chest as she tried to hold on, to keep her head above water. But she wasn't sure she could. The assault of sensations was so swift, so intense, she felt dizzy inside and out. When his teeth nipped her bottom lip, she released a shaky exhale. But the moment she went to inhale again, his lips were on hers, his tongue doing masterful things to a mouth that had only been kissed two other times before.

Live in the moment.

Her dress was short, so it took absolutely no effort for Jackson's hand to slip under the soft, flowing

material and past the ban of her thong. His strong
fingers were touching her swollen flesh in the next
second and her eyes shot open. She froze and so did he.

"Did I hurt you? Are you alright?" he was asking
instantly, but she could not reply.

She blinked and blinked, but could not see him.
Instead she saw a dark room—her mother on one side
and Jana on the other, the Bible and the knife that cut
deep into her best friend's skin. She could hear a
choking sound but had no idea it was her, could hear a
name being called over and over again, but at the
moment didn't know who Tara was.

So much for living in the moment.

(⌇)

"You're sure you're okay?" Jack asked after they'd
arrived at the restaurant and she'd taken a few seconds
to freshen up in the ladies' room.

A few seconds had been more like 15 minutes and
he'd been just about to go in there and get her, when
she'd finally appeared. The memory of her face going
totally ashen the second he touched her plump, wet
folds would be permanently emblazoned in his
memory. When she'd begun to choke, he'd had no idea
what to do, and that, for Jack Carrington, had never
happened before. It appeared this woman was pulling
all types of firsts out of him tonight.

"I'm fine," she said quickly, her lips even lifting
slightly into a partial smile.

It was a pretty look, even if it wasn't genuine. The
moment she opened the bathroom door and he saw that
her hair was pulled back into that bun, he'd wanted to
frown. No, he'd wanted to run his finger through what
he was sure were soft as silk tresses, releasing it from
its bindings and watching it flow around her shoulders.
The blue dress she wore was shades lighter than his
shirt, but fit the line of her body as if it had been made

specifically for her. And the shoes, he'd already decided she could keep them on, even once he had her naked.

That, coupled with the kiss in the car, the feel of her hot, wet skin beneath his fingers after he'd slipped his hand under her dress, made Jack think he just might have a coronary if he didn't get buried inside her soon.

But then there had been that look and she'd gone still and he'd thought for one second that he might have hurt her in some way. All he could think about was fixing whatever he'd done wrong. He'd quickly moved her from his lap, adjusting her clothes and talking to her so that he was sure she hadn't died in his arms. The thought was ridiculous, he knew, but he'd thought it anyway. After a few moments, she'd spoken to him in a shy, distant voice, saying the same thing she'd just said. "I'm fine."

"I ordered you a glass of wine. If you don't like red, I can order you something else," he told her after helping Tara into her seat and moving around the table to sit across from her.

He should have booked a private booth. He wanted to be close to her again, to feel her warmth beside him, to keep her safe. This time Jack had to shake his head at himself. What was he thinking? Keeping her safe? Keeping her close? She was a woman that he was attracted to, case closed. All this other nonsense was crowding his mind, fogging his focus. He picked up his glass, taking a quick gulp of his vodka and cranberry before looking to her again.

She was sitting with her back ramrod straight as if the chair were now somehow hurting her. She obviously liked red wine because she was just putting her glass down as well.

"Red is my favorite," she told him when she looked up to see him staring.

"Good," he said, expelling the breath he hadn't been aware he was holding.

Minutes later they ordered and Jack had begun to relax significantly, almost to the point of feeling like his old self again.

"Tell me something else you like," he asked, wanting to hear everything there was to know about her.

Her eyes grew a little wider as she looked from the menu she'd just handed to the waiter back to him. He could see that his request had been unexpected, because she blinked, and then cleared her throat, flattening her hands on the table before responding.

"I like to read and to sing in the shower," she replied. "How about you?"

Jack chuckled before he could catch himself. "I'm not a sing in the shower type of guy. And I read so many contracts throughout the day, the last thing I want to see when I go home are words on paper."

"That's not telling me what you like," she insisted.

Every now and then he'd see that glimpse of spunk in her and, surprisingly, found he liked it. Normally he didn't have a chance to figure out if there was something about a woman he liked or disliked. Nor had he ever cared, thinking only about if her looks and talent could culminate in a thoroughly pleasing release. And yet, here he was, asking Tara questions and being more interested in her answers than he was in the contracts waiting for him to review back at his condo.

"I like fast cars and lucrative business deals that don't go smoothly," he told her honestly.

One elegantly arched eyebrow lifted. "That's different. I prefer my work go as smoothly as possible."

"Where's the challenge in that?" he asked her. "The best part of my job is the negotiation process, or the battle as some in my office like to call it."

"Only a person who always wins the battle would say that," was her reply.

She kept her gaze level with his, even though her voice had taken on a more sullen tone with that last statement.

"Sometimes it's not about winning, but the fact that you showed up for the fight in the first place that counts," he said. It was a strange thing to say since Jack never lost. He was an astute businessman that waited until the perfect moment to pounce on an unsuspecting or knowingly floundering company. At that point, there's really no point in fighting the inevitable. Yet, some business owners, the best of them, in Jack's estimation, carry on until the bitter end. He respected them so much more for their final efforts than he did the others who immediately rolled over to concede.

Their dinner arrived and the conversation shifted to his grilled pork chops and her steak salad. She really did like the wine because when the waiter walked by she asked for another glass. Her dog's name was Vicious and she was Tara's best friend, a sad, yet true statement, Jack assessed. She'd been in Seal Beach for only a year having moved from the East Coast— something he already knew but was pleased that she'd told him.

However, she didn't tell him where on the East Coast, nor did she bring up that night at The Corporation in New York.

Jack wondered why.

"So, what made you come out to The Corporation the other night?"

He'd decided to wait a little longer before bringing up New York. Truth be told, he wanted her to remember seeing him there, wanted her to remember sitting on his lap and offering herself to him before running out. He remembered it with such startlingly clarity, he could admit if only to himself. The fact that she didn't stung just a bit.

She finished chewing the last bite of chocolate decadence cake she'd had for dessert and wiped her hands on her napkin before replying.

"I don't know."

It was a simple as that. Jack frowned because it was also a lie.

"I go there frequently. I've never seen you at this location," he said slowly, watching for any new change to her demeanor. It seemed that with each question he'd proposed she either readily answered, or cowered in some way before rebounding with what she thought was a suitable response. She was definitely hiding something. What was really strange was how bothered Jack was because of it.

"It was just one of those things. I found the visitor card and figured why not," she continued nonchalantly. She'd even gone so far as to shrug her shoulders to make the comment appear more genuine.

Jack still didn't believe her. But the waiter arrived with the check and his cell phone rang and he knew the moment to press the matter was lost.

He gave the waiter his credit card and excused himself from the table to take the call. Five minutes later he was back, frowning and not at all happy.

"Unfortunately, we'll have to end the night here," he told her. "Mercer will take you home."

She looked confused and he didn't blame her, but neither could he explain further.

"I'd like to see you again," he stated after he'd helped her out of her chair and they were heading out the door where his car was already waiting at the curb.

"I don't know," was her immediate response.

He probably should have expected it, but he had no intention of taking that as her final answer. He wanted to see her again, to touch her and taste her, and so much more. Jack turned then, cupping her face in his palms as he bent down, licking a heated line across the seam of her lips. She was looking up at him, blinking in surprise, and his body tightened. She wanted more, he could see it as clear as day. So he obliged.

Again he licked her lips until she gasped and his tongue took the opportunity to plunge deep. He kissed hungrily, quenching a thirst he hadn't even known existed. She kissed him back, tilting her head as much as his hold on her would allow, but never touching him. When she whimpered into his mouth, he wanted to pick her up and carry her to the car, to lay her on the soft leather back seats and fuck her until she whimpered and gasped again, until she was whispering his name.

He pulled away instead, realizing only in that instant that they were standing outside on a very public street, kissing like two horny teenagers. It was a great opportunity for the paparazzi that normally followed him like a pack of dogs. He'd probably confused them tonight by using a driver and a different car than was his normal routine. Still, he shouldn't have taken a gamble that there was no one around to exploit his one moment of weakness.

"I'll call you tomorrow," he whispered over her lips, his gaze locking with hers.

Their eyes had remained open during the kiss, almost as if they were both afraid to close them, afraid to end the moment with that seemingly inconsequential action.

Tara didn't respond, but hurriedly looked away from him and made her way to the car. Jack stood there entranced after the Phantom had pulled away from the curb. The incessant blowing of a horn finally yanked him away from thoughts of her in his arms and in his bed.

Straightening his tie, he walked hurriedly to the SUV that had summoned him and opened the back passenger door, climbing quickly inside.

CHAPTER SIX

Lust is sin and sin is death.

Doris Leigh's voice greeted Tara the moment she lay in her bed. She would not sleep. Considering only an hour ago she'd returned from what she considered her first date, ever, she hadn't really expected to get much rest tonight. Still, this wasn't the voice she wanted in her head right now, and those weren't the words she needed to hear.

Turning onto her side, Tara tried to shut out the all too familiar voice and the scolding tone. She bunched her pillow beneath her head and closed her eyes, trying to recall the tender steak she'd eaten earlier, the rich chocolate of the decadent cake, the smooth mellow tartness of the wine as it ran along her tongue, down her throat. And the way he smelled. She inhaled deeply and exhaled, remembering Jack.

In the next moment her mind flipped all the way back to her sophomore year in high school when she gave Lyle Tamrin her virginity.

Lyle sat behind her in English class. He'd had great lips, not too full and not too thin. His skin was an olive complexion, rumored to be from his Greek grandmother. His hair on his head and along his muscled arms was dark, alluring. His eyes were blue, almost like the pictures of the Caribbean Sea from that travel brochure she loved to peruse whenever Doris Leigh wasn't around.

He was tall with broad shoulders and a wide chest. He was her high school crush. And the funny thing was that he'd liked her to. She'd thought that was weird since she wasn't a cheerleader and didn't attend any of his basketball games and, aside from English, he never saw her during or outside of school.

"I could come over and help you study for the exam," he'd told her one spring day after class.

His t-shirt was tight against his chest, his jeans fitting his taut buttocks and thighs. She hadn't been able to stare at much more than his body as her mind wrapped itself around the fact that he'd stopped to talk to her.

"I get better grades than you," she'd finally replied, giving him a tentative smile.

He smiled back and she'd felt the world tilt around her.

"That's true. Then I could come over and you could help me study," was the counteroffer.

His fingers touched her chin and then moved in a slow line along the ridge of her lower lip. Her entire body tingled, her fingers itching to do to him what he was doing to her, but not knowing how or if she should.

She shouldn't. She knew that. Doris Leigh had warned her about boys and about touching them, wanting them. Melanie already knew she should be moving away and heading down the hallway, as far from Lyle Tamrin as she could get.

Yet, she hadn't turned away, hadn't even blinked for that matter because she was afraid if she did he would disappear and she'd realize she was actually dreaming. But Lyle moved closer until the hard tips of her nipples had rubbed against his six pack. It was a delicious sensation that coursed through her body at that moment, one she felt compelled to explore.

"I want to be alone with you. Don't you want me too?"

Again, the right answer was on the tip of her tongue, but she'd replied instead, "Yes. I want you...too."

Later that afternoon, Lyle was at her house and they'd sat close on the living room couch. It was an old and ugly couch, with dark red pineapples on its dingy beige background. The carpet was also grimy and the television set—the one Doris Leigh forbid anyone from ever touching—could only get three channels clearly. She hated her house, was embarrassed sometimes to even live here. Doris Leigh didn't work. She received government assistance, saying she deserved it after enduring all she had from that "good for nothing man." That's what Doris Leigh had called her daughter's father so often, his real name just about forgotten. So her mother cleaned during the day and went to church for most of the night. And the house continued to look the same.

Lyle didn't seem to notice as he was too busy unbuttoning her blouse. His calloused fingers were rough against her skin, but she didn't complain because the intimate contact was new and different and deliciously arousing. The bra she was wearing was too small because Doris Leigh didn't believe in spending money on frivolous things—and yes, she thought wearing the proper sized underwear, and sometimes even clothes, was frivolous. It was another thing Lyle didn't notice because as soon as the bra was off, his head lowered and he was dragging his tongue over her exposed flesh. She'd sucked in a breath and then another as his tongue had touched her young nipples and then she'd felt lightheaded.

He'd mumbled something about being greedy and great tits, but words weren't really what she'd wanted to comprehend then. Her body seemed to hum all over, like there was some kind of button that Lyle had switched on inside her. The area between her legs was throbbing. She knew that's where he was heading, where this entire supposed study session was going. She'd learned about it in health class even though Doris Leigh hadn't signed the form saying she could take sex education. She'd forged it herself and sat in the class eager to learn what her mother so despised about the act.

"I can't wait to fuck you," Lyle had said candidly.

She didn't mention that she couldn't wait either. She also didn't ask if he had a condom, even though safe sex had been one of the first things covered in health class. Instead she'd begun to undress herself while watching from the corner of her eye as Lyle tore his clothes off too. He lifted one of her legs, pushing it up onto the back of the sofa. Then he moved the other one until it was dangling off the edge. He'd licked his lips then and knelt on the couch thrusting two fingers between her legs. She'd bit her tongue to keep from screaming out in pain and because he was actually groaning as he moved his finger inside of her.

"Next time I'll taste you," he said when she'd started to get used to feeling him down there.

"I'll taste you and then I'll fuck you," he continued.

She hadn't been real sure of what he'd meant by tasting her. He was grabbing his erection, and she couldn't keep her eyes on that and try to figure out what his words meant, so she stopped trying.

He'd pushed what felt like the whole length of himself into her in the next second and that time she did yell out. Lyle acted as if he hadn't heard her and pulled back, pushing himself even deeper into her this time.

She didn't want to yell again, but she had started to feel like maybe this wasn't the right way to be doing this. Maybe it was...

"Tramp! Slut! Whore!" the words vibrated off the walls of the small house. "May God have mercy on your soul!"

Doris Leigh was home from Bible study early and all hell was literally about to break loose. Lyle had been yanked off her as her mother had spat more scriptures, at the same time threatening to call the police on the boy. She'd wondered why since having consensual sex wasn't a crime, but asking wouldn't have made any difference. In Doris Leigh's mind anything that had to do with sex was off limits. It was sacrilege and the righteous believer was intent on bringing that message home loud and clear.

"God is not pleased," had been the last words Doris said to her that night after she'd whipped her with a leather belt as if she'd stolen something instead of having simply given away her virginity.

She'd been so angry and in so much pain that night she hadn't been able to cry, hadn't even considered it. All she'd wanted to do then was disappear.

Overall, as it turned out, she figured sex with a boy wasn't something she'd wanted to repeat. Yet, the urgings were still there. And eventually, she would learn to assuage them by watching.

Ultimately, that pleasure would also turn on her.

Tara huffed, rolling over to her other side, blinking at the wall for endless moments hoping to rid herself of the horrid memories before attempting to fall asleep once more. She had no idea how much time passed before she realized it was futile. Looking over she saw that her dog was on the same, sleepless page, sitting up on her own bed, staring directly at Tara while wagging her tail.

It was just about midnight and Tara was walking along the beach, Vicious running up ahead, barking exuberantly. The dog had been more than irritable ever since Tara had come home tonight. Maybe it was because Tara had left her alone while she'd gone out with Jackson. Ove the last year they'd been virtually inseparable so Tara figured that was as good an excuse as any for the hyper behavior. She also wanted to believe it was guilt that had her walking along the beach this time of night, letting Vicious run wild. And not the horrid memories from her past.

A breeze blew and she crossed her arms over her shoulders, shivering in the cool night air, her toes curling in the sand as the sound of crashing waves echoed in the background. She inhaled deeply, trying to clear her mind. It was no use, she was still giddy from her date. It had been her first and she knew she would cherish the memory forever. What girl wouldn't love being picked up in a fancy car and driven to an even fancier restaurant with a handsome and debonair man? None that she knew of, she thought with a huge grin spreading across her face.

Dinner had been very tasty, for the moments that she'd actually concentrated on the food, instead of trying not to stare dreamily at Jackson. It was hard not to be amazed by his charisma. The way he walked into a room and commanded all attention, and not only from the staff that were clearly bending over backwards to do his bidding. But the other guests who had been seemingly enjoying their meal until they arrived. Then all heads had turned to them as they made their way to the table, and while they ate Tara had seen several of them turning in their seats to stare over at Jackson. They would whisper and smile and she remembered feeling a bit overwhelmed by how popular he apparently was.

Of course he'd acted as if it was nothing, but that was just his way. Jackson Carrington never seemed bothered by anything. To the contrary, whatever was said or done he took in stride. No, that's not correct, because at one point he had called the manager over, whispering something in the older gentlemen's ear. There was no more staring or smiling coming their way from that point on. Just like that he'd put a stop to it and in that moment she wondered if there were anything this man wanted that he could not get.

He wanted her.

Those three words were new to Tara, but even with her troubled background, she wasn't naïve enough to think about ignoring that fact. What had shocked her was how much she wanted him as well. The urge to have sex with a man had been quieted long ago and she hadn't entertained any thoughts of it over the years. She'd been satisfied with what her sex life entailed, enjoying that rise and fall of anticipation and the pleasure it brought her. She was content.

Until now.

The sound of the waves and the steady gust of breeze pulled Tara from her thoughts and she searched for Vicious up ahead. The silly dog had run off the beach and was on the compounded sand patch leading beneath the pier. They'd walked too far, she thought with a frown and it was late and she should get back.

In seconds fear had laced its way up her spine, chilling the warm thoughts she'd been having about Jackson and their time together tonight. She walked faster, calling out to Vicious so they could hurry and turn back. But Vicious didn't heed her calls. She could still see her but the dog was staring straight ahead as if it saw something that Tara did not. She broke into a run at that point, wanting to hurry back into the house and out of this ominous darkness.

Just as she was within reaching distance of Vicious, strong arms wrapped around her waist lifting her off her feet. She opened her mouth to scream but a hand clamped down over it. Fight or flight instinct kicked in immediately and she started to kick and squirm, and then she stopped.

His tongue licked along the line of her ear, dipping quickly inside while his thick erection pressed persistently into the crevice of her bottom. She closed her eyes and inhaled, and stayed still in his arms. How she knew it was Jackson or what he was doing out here, she would never know, but she didn't dare move, especially after he whispered, "Keep still and keep quiet."

The words could have been intimidating, or possibly deadly, considering the circumstances that had brought her to this place, but Tara felt none of the fear she'd known that night of the murder and subsequent nights after. No, at this moment all she felt was heat swirling up and throughout her body, melting her against him.

Jackson loosened his grip on her slightly as he carried her past the wooden beams under the pier. It was even darker here, secluded from anyone else walking along the beach. Her heart pattered quickly, her breasts swelling, center throbbing. She felt surrounded, cocooned in strength and sex appeal that was threatening to suffocate her. As if he'd read her mind, Jackson let her feet touch the ground and moved his hand from her mouth, but kept his one arm around her waist.

"I didn't want to leave you earlier," he told her, his voice gruff and warm against her ear. "So I had to come back."

"How did you know I was out here?" she asked, praying he wouldn't hear how nervous she was.

"You like the beach," he replied. "That's why you moved to this location. It's where you walk your dog and gain some solace. Am I correct?"

All the while he talked Jackson's hand had flattened on her torso, moving slowly down until now he was cupping her juncture through the yoga pants she'd changed into. Tara trembled. She couldn't help it. Then she licked her lips and took a deep breath in an effort to calm herself.

"You're right," she whispered. "I like the beach."

"And you like me touching you," he continued, reaching farther between her legs until she had no other option but to bend her knees slightly, opening her thighs to grant him access.

Tara shook her head. It was dark out here and she couldn't see. She could feel. Oh damn, was she feeling a myriad of sensations with his touch and the sound of his voice. But she wanted to see him. She tried to turn but he held her firm.

"Tell me you like me touching you," he stated.

No. He ordered and a ripple of desire traveled straight to her pussy.

Tara swallowed and tried to say the words, tried to imagine how a normal female would react. She couldn't, because she wasn't normal.

"Let me go," she told him. "Please."

For a moment she didn't think he would, but then his hand slipped from between her legs and the warmth that had sheltered her was lost. With the next breeze she actually shivered before turning to face him. His silhouette was big and broad, his facial features barely discernable.

"What do you want from me?" she asked after seconds of unbearable silence.

Jackson slipped his hands into his pockets and waited. Then he removed one hand and moved his fingers in a gesture telling her to come closer. She took a tentative step and then another, until she was standing in front of him, her body longing for that warmth once more.

"I want to give you what you need," he told her simply. "Any and everything you need, Tara. I want to be the one who supplies it for you."

"Why?"

"Because you intrigue me and I am not easily intrigued," he responded. "Because my body reacts to yours in a way that it's never reacted to another woman before. Because I want you."

And he always got what he wanted. He didn't say that but the words hung in the air like a solemn declaration of truth. She had to swallow hard again to let that fact settle in her mind.

"What if I don't want you?" she asked him. What if she couldn't want him, or any man, ever?

With his free hand Jackson reached for her wrist. He guided her hand to his crotch, letting her fingers settle over his rigid length. He was hard and hot and thick and long and her mouth watered with the thought.

"Tell me you don't want me now."

She closed her eyes, her fingers still cupping him, her mind at war with her body. In her head were too many voices—Doris Leigh's, Jana's, Melanie's. She shook her head with despair, but she didn't pull her hand away and she didn't open her eyes.

"I want to see," she said, not sure she'd spoken aloud, until he replied.

"Go ahead. Look at what you want."

When she didn't move and still didn't open her eyes, Tara felt him moving her hand to the side and heard the sound of him unzipping his pants. She licked her lips, heart hammering in her chest, eyes still closed.

"Look, Tara."

She wanted to, damn did she want to, but her eyes wouldn't open. Not until Jackson leaned in, touching his lips to first one closed lid and then the other. "Look," he whispered again.

She trembled, her lids struggling to open, her hands shaking. She had to see, that's what she did. She looked and she got off and then she was done. Why was now different? Why couldn't she simply look at him?

There was no reason. She could and, dammit, she would.

With a quick motion Tara took a step back and opened her eyes. She looked down at his length, jutting forward.

"Touch me, Tara."

Again, it wasn't a request. She should say no to his commanding tone and get the hell out of here. This was all just too weird. Where had this man come from and why her? Why now? She had enough to worry about, she didn't need this. And yet, Tara knew instinctively that she did.

She touched him, without any further prodding or doubting. Wrapping her palm around his length, she closed her fingers and sighed. He was warm and hard and her thighs trembled. She was wet, the thin strip of her thong pressing—now annoyingly—between the plump folds of her vagina. She put both hands on him then, letting one hand slip to the top while the other immediately went to the base of his arousal. She stroked and stroked and he simply stood there, strong and stoic almost as if he weren't effected at all. But when she looked up at him, when she could see his eyes grow darker, even with the night surrounding them, she knew he'd spoken the truth. He did want her.

And she wanted…

"I have to go," she said abruptly pulling her hands away from him. "Vicious!" she called to her dog again after completely forgetting about her while fondling this guy under a dark pier.

She was out in the open again before Jackson spoke.

"I'll walk you home," he told her.

"I don't need you to," she said over her shoulder, noting that his glorious package was no longer on display.

"I'll do it anyway," he said coming up beside her. "Don't argue, it won't change my mind."

Tara had opened her mouth to do just that, then clamped her lips closed at his response. "Fine," she muttered and refused to say another word to him for the duration of the walk.

She'd been about to go into her house when he grabbed her at the waist again. This time she was facing him, her head instantly tilting back so she could look into his face and not the broadness of his chest.

"I still want to be the one to give you what you need, Tara. All you have to do is tell me what that is."

She had started to shake her head, when he shook his instead. "No. Don't deny me or yourself. When you're ready, tell me what you want and I'll make sure you have it."

When she opened her mouth to reply Jackson silenced her with a kiss. His tongue slipping quickly inside her mouth, sparring expertly with hers. One of his hands cupping the back of her neck, tilting her head so that he could deepen the kiss. He pulled away as quickly as he'd begun, turning and disappearing down the walkway.

Tara didn't think she could move a muscle, could barely comprehend what the hell had just happened. But she did move, pride kicking in and she went inside her house, falling back against the door and letting out the breath she'd been holding since his lips touched hers.

When she felt her legs were stable enough Tara went upstairs, Vicious trotting right behind her. She entered her bedroom and headed for the small antique desk she'd ordered online and that fit perfectly with the distressed wood of her bedroom set. Her laptop was there, right where she'd left it after working all day long.

In the last five minutes she'd made up her mind. Or was it during the last seconds of that mouthwatering kiss? She wasn't sure, but she knew it had to be now or never. There was something she could do to move past the awful memories, to be the person she truly wanted to be, to reach for what she'd been told so many times was unobtainable.

The boot up was quick and before any thoughts of changing her mind could surface, her inbox appeared. When she'd come in earlier tonight, the first thing she'd done was stuff the card Jack had given her during dinner under her pillow. It was a habit she'd developed while under witness protection. This was the place she would hide stuff that she didn't want the marshals to see. Tara had no idea if the marshals really went through her things when she wasn't looking, but she figured it might be a part of keeping her safe from herself. But she wasn't a suicide risk, regardless of what that ridiculously inept psychiatrist had told them when she'd first come here.

She got up and went to the bed to retrieve the card, then hurriedly came back. For endless seconds she stared at it looking over the embossed black lettering, even touching it as if she thought it might at some point disappear.

JACKSON CARRINGTON, CEO Carrington
Enterprises
Lake View Towers, 18th Floor, Beverly Hills
90212

It went on to list his office telephone number and email. When she flipped it over, there was another telephone number and email, handwritten. Personal information, she guessed.

Propping the card on the laptop she touched her fingers to the keyboard and hesitated only a second before typing in the email address—the personal one.

Hello Jack

She began the message.

I like to watch. What do you like to do at The Corporation?

She signed the message with a simple "T" after typing the question, logged out of her email and closed the laptop. After closing down the laptop she carried the card with her back to her bed, this time slipping it into her pillow case. Then she lay back on the bed, pulling the sheets over her legs and closing her eyes.

Jackson had asked her what she wanted. Told her all she had to do was tell him what she needed and she had. Feeling proud, she closed her eyes knowing that Tara Sullivan would have a new and full life regardless of what had taken place in the past with her mother and with Jana and even with over-excited Lyle who had never spoken to her after that day at her house.

꧁ ꧂

She was a whoring bitch, just like all the rest of the whoring bitches in the world. He despised them all, knowing without any doubt they were only good for the tits and ass they were blessed with.

Right from the start he'd known she was no different, no matter what she said or how she pretended like she didn't really know what had been going on around her. She knew alright, just like her friend knew. They were both whores, going to that sex club in New York all dressed up and ready to get fucked. Well, they had, at least one of them anyway. The other had only watched, perverted tramp that she was. But it was all a cover. She wanted to get it hard and hot too, that's why she'd gone to that same club in Beverly Hills. She was hot for it and he was going to give it to her.

After that he'd be rid of the bitch, once and for all.

CHAPTER SEVEN

"It's a U.S. Marshal car," Trent informed him. "Any information beyond that is of course going to be classified. I'll have to do some digging."

"It's probably nothing," Jack said, sitting back in his office chair, fingers gliding over his chin, contemplating Trent's words.

"You just noticed the car this morning?" Trent asked.

"Right. It was parked in front of my building. I noticed it when I pulled out of the garage because it was early. The sun hadn't come up yet and as soon as I turned out, the headlights to the sedan came on. I recognized the same car again about two blocks away, and that's when I sent you the message and the tag number."

Jack replayed the events in his mind as he spoke. He hadn't slept well last night, images of Tara Sullivan touching him out on the beach occupying his thoughts even as another woman's shrill and manipulative voice echoed in his mind.

Soleil Ducovney was indeed back in town, and the first thing she'd done was call a meeting of her favorite men, the Carrington brothers. Jerald had apparently received her call early last evening and immediately notified Jason and then Jack. He'd showed up at the restaurant after having picked Jason up at the airport, coming back from his trip to Las Vegas. Jason and his wife Celise were going to visit the senior Carringtons before continuing on to their home in Monterey. Jerald's call and the following impromptu meeting at Spago had rerouted everyone's plans.

During the ride, Jerald had explained the call he received in these simple words:

"She's lost her fucking mind!" he screamed in the cabin of the SUV that he drove for the express purpose of keeping their privacy.

"There's nothing she can do to hurt any of us," Jason stated calmly. "None of us ever slept with her. This leverage she thinks she has is nothing but bullshit."

It was odd that the youngest of the brothers was so composed and indifferent while the middle one was speeding through the streets of Beverly Hills, cursing every other car that dared be on the road with him. Jack, on the other hand, continued to recall every word Jerald had said to him on the phone.

"Soleil's back and she's demanding millions to keep quiet about the Carrington secrets."

Jack had asked what she'd meant by that and instead Jerald had said he was on his way. Jack obliged because Jerald sounded as if he were close to killing someone— preferably Soleil Ducovney.

"She's just trying to get attention and unfortunately, we're about to give it to her," Jack finally replied in response to Jason's statement.

"I don't understand why we're doing that either," Jason said from the passenger seat where he was giving Jerald a side look.

"She knows something," Jerald told them. "Soleil doesn't bluff. She doesn't have to. And whatever it is, it's explosive."

"Unless she's having dad's baby I wouldn't consider it explosive, Jerald," Jason replied dryly.

Jack sat in the backseat and remained silent. It was true that he'd never slept with Soleil, but she had been to The Corporation. She'd come as a guest of some record exec she'd been dating at the time. And she'd seen Jack there. He'd been sitting in his favorite spot indulging in his favorite drink when she'd sauntered over to him and asked to go to his room. He'd respectfully declined and she'd been livid. A week later she'd showed up at his office wearing nothing but a trench coat and he'd had security escort her from the building. Never, not in his wildest dreams, would he have assumed she would open her mouth about seeing him there, but right at this moment, there was a ball of dread sitting in his gut that warned that's exactly what this little meeting was about.

When they'd arrived at the restaurant, Soleil wasn't there. Jerald had continued to curse, while Jason called his wife to tell her he was on his way back. Jack had stood, staring blankly, thinking of how he planned to deal with Soleil and keep his life and his family's reputation intact.

How those thoughts had led him to Tara's house, Jack had no idea. But after another arousing interlude with her, he'd finally returned home, poured a drink and sat down in his favorite chair, staring out at the Beverly Hills skyline the way he liked to do. He thought of her again, because no matter what else was going on, she occupied his mind as if she were the most important issue to be dealt with. He wasn't sure that was the case, but for the rest of the night it was useless trying to think of anything else.

"I wanted to come in early to look over the contract language for this new deal," he continued talking to Trent because he realized he'd been silent for far too long. "When I arrived at work and turned into this garage, I was leaning out to swipe my ID when I saw the sedan again. It passed the entrance of the building, stopping just down the street before the light."

"And it's still out there now?" Trent asked.

Jack stood from his chair, going to the window and looking down. The Lake View Towers was a 20-story high-rise office complex in the center of Beverly Hills. Carrington Enterprises had leased three floors in the building for the last 15 years. From Jack's office, he had an unfettered view of downtown Los Angeles and the Hollywood Hills. This morning he could also see down to the street where the black sedan was parked at the corner in front of a FedEx truck.

"Yes. It's still out there," he reported.

"You piss anyone off lately?"

Trent's question tore Jack's gaze from the window as he turned back toward his desk, his expression grim. Immediately he thought of Soleil's threat, but quickly dismissed it. No way was Soleil mixed up with the U.S. Marshals.

"What kind of question is that? I'm a businessman."

Trent chuckled. "You're the head of a company that buys other companies and sells them off piece by piece, regardless of the fact that it may have been someone's dream, their life's work. I'm sure there are more than a few people who don't like that so much. Not to mention you're a filthy rich bachelor with very eccentric tastes when it comes to your sex life. So I'll ask again, have you pissed anyone off lately?"

Of course Trent Donovan would know about The Corporation. The man was notoriously thorough in his work, and for as many times as Jack had been to his house, sat at a dinner table with his gorgeous wife Tia and held their son Trevor in his arms, he figured a background check on him had been a given. But up until this moment, Trent had never mentioned anything he may have found on his look into Jack's life.

Jack wasn't sure how he felt about it being brought up now.

"Like I said, I'm a businessman, in every aspect of my life. I deal with everyone on a professional level. I keep it clean, short and sweet. Get in and get out."

"Right," Trent replied. "I know what you mean. And I basically agree with you on that end. But if you've picked up a tail and one that's connected to the U.S. Marshal's office, something not so clear-cut is going on."

Sitting back in his chair Jack sighed. "I agree. So what now?"

"I'll make a couple of calls to see if I can come up with some connection to you or your company."

"The deal I'm working on now, a few of the board members are Malaysian. It's a trade company which originated overseas but merged with another entity in Miami about five years ago. Our takeover would be global," he told Trent. This wasn't usually information Jack would give out, especially since the deal hadn't been finalized yet. But if he was on some type of federal watch list because of the international dealings, he wanted to know sooner rather than later.

"I've got someone in with the Feds. I can give him a call too, just to see if there's any ongoing investigation. Text me the names of all the board members," Trent told him. "On second thought, don't text. Write the names and connections down on a piece of paper. I'll pick it up at The Sunset."

It took Jack a second to comprehend, but when he did his reply was quick. "Done," he told him before disconnecting the call.

Only a member of the elite would know there was a suite called The Sunset, and only someone who had looked deep in Jack's background would know that The Sunset was reserved especially for him.

Placing his cell phone in the center of the desk blotter, Jack stared at it for a few seconds. If Trent didn't want him to text, he obviously thought there was something to this sedan sitting outside. Thoughts of some international investigation stuck in his head and he cursed. This was a multibillion dollar deal. The last thing he needed was for it to fall apart.

Jack wasn't one to worry. His motto had always been to find out the problem and implement a solution, which was exactly what he'd begun to do with Soleil. Additionally, he reached for the notepad sitting beside his desktop and grabbed a pen from the leather holder that matched all the other accessories on his desk and began making his list.

About 30 minutes later a black Navigator was waiting to take him to The Corporation. If the person in that government vehicle had followed him here this morning, he'd be looking for the Jaguar to come cruising out of the parking garage.

Pushing through the tinted glass doors leading to the marble reception booth, Jack entered the facility. For all intent and purposes, it looked like a normal business except there was no nameplate at the front doors or over the reception area. All a person would see upon entering would be endless black marble fixtures amidst the dark cranberry colored carpet and the smiling face of the day receptionist named Cheyenne.

"Hello Mr. Carrington," Cheyenne greeted him.

Upon entering the building, guests of The Corporation gained entrance to an underground garage by using their membership cards at the security gate. Swiping that card immediately alerted the receptionist to who was arriving.

"Hello, Cheyenne. I'm going upstairs for a few minutes," he told her.

She nodded, her coal black hair hanging down her back, straight as an arrow, shifting only slightly with her movement.

"Will you need any assistance?" she asked.

And by assistance she was referring to Adonna.

"No. Not today," he replied tightly.

Since the last time he'd been here, Jack hadn't been able to think about Adonna or any other woman that he'd slept with in the past. The mere mention of her name had his gut churning, as if he were somehow repulsed but had no idea why. He moved quickly to the elevator that would take him to the penthouse suites. His ID card opened the door and he slipped inside, the rich scent of leather immediately assailing him. The sitting area was full of wine colored Italian leather, from the couch to the base of the lamps.

Jack didn't bother with the lights. The room darkening blinds had been lifted so that sunlight poured in through the floor-to-ceiling windows. He moved to the desk and placed the envelope he'd brought from his office into the top drawer. Just as he was about to turn around and leave, his phone vibrated in his jacket pocket and he reached for it.

It was only notifications. When he'd awakened this morning, he'd had to turn his phone on and off because it wasn't updating as fast as it should have been. With a frown he thought to remind DeMarco, his assistant, to make a call to his provider sometime this week because the mobile still apparently wasn't updating correctly. He'd received 111 new messages in his personal email box since last night.

Frowning down at the device, he opened the email app and waited while the messages downloaded. He watched without too much interest because only his family members, a few old college friends and, of course, the spammers of the world had his personal email address. He doubted there was anything he really needed to see, but always checked just to be sure.

And today, he thought as his heart picked up its rhythmic beat, he was glad he'd checked. He read Tara's message and immediately replied:

I like control. Would you like to watch me use that control?

Tara had read Jack's reply to her message more than 20 times in the last 10 minutes. She'd been sitting at her desk in her bedroom, not really working on the project she had on the screen but daydreaming instead.

She'd sat down four hours ago with the intention of getting lots of work done. That hadn't actually happened as she'd been extremely distracted. She'd been wondering about the email she sent last night. Would Jackson Carrington answer her? Would he think she was some type of flake and ignore her? Would he detest her preferences and mock her the way she figured Emilio wanted to do on a daily basis?

Back and forth she'd tortured herself with doubt and recriminations. And then he'd replied.

The message box had popped up onto her screen, the pinging sound she'd programmed for notifications jolting her from the work she should have been doing.

Now she couldn't decide how to respond or if she should respond. Her heart hammered in her chest as another war of indecision began. Just as she was about to put her fingers on the keyboard and attempt to reply to him, she heard a noise. Tara jumped in her chair as if someone had caught her stealing. Frowning she watched as Vicious came trotting into the room to plop down on her bed that sat just beneath the window.

"Silly dog," she chided, and then turned her attention back to the screen.

He liked control.

She thought about that for a moment, wondering if he meant that he was a dom and he was looking for a sub. If so, she didn't think she was up for that. Being a voyeur, a deviant to some, Tara had made it a point to know as much as she could about others like her. Not just voyeurs, but those who practiced a different sexual lifestyle. It made her feel like she was a part of something different and special, maybe, not the odd man out as her mother had predicted she would be.

Yet, the remnants of Doris Leigh's demented biblical teachings still rung loud and clear in her mind. Tara knew Doris Leigh was narcissistic, nobody had to tell her that. Still, she had been her mother, and there was a big part of any woman that either tried to be like her mother or at least seek validation from the first female role model in her life. Unfortunately, Tara had a sucky role model whose only attempt at shaping her daughter's future had been to destroy it.

Taking a deep breath, she left Doris Leigh in the background of her mind and replied to the message.

Yes. I would like for you to show me how you control.

She typed the reply and hit send before any mind changing could take place. Then she sat back in her chair and waited.

The wait did not take long.

9pm The Sunset Room

He wanted her to come to The Corporation again. She already knew she would go, just as she told herself this time there would be no running out, no letting the past get to her. This time, she would be Tara Sullivan, no matter what the cost.

CHAPTER EIGHT

The day had been a busy one for Jack. He'd spent the bulk of it at the club after making a call to Lauren Asby, from Infinity Interior Designs, the firm he'd used for his condo. If Tara were coming here tonight, he wanted the place to have a totally different look, to have a design no woman before Tara had seen or experienced.

Throughout the morning there was a flurry of activity as furniture was moved out and new pieces brought in. The heavy oak and traditional pieces were gone. In were more contemporary chairs, a new bedroom set, linens and new rugs. Lauren had frowned at the request for mirrors, but Jack had ignored her. He knew what he wanted, knew what Tara needed.

At noon he had a lunch date that could not be broken so he'd left, traveling all the way to Santa Monica and back. When he returned the envelope he'd placed in the desk drawer was gone. He thought with satisfaction how thorough and discreet Trent Donovan was.

While there was really no need for him to stay at The Corporation to oversee the continuation of the redesign, Jack did not leave. Lauren was excellent at her job and he trusted her implicitly, still the importance of tonight—even if he were still trying to convince himself that it was a normal change—was too high for him to walk away. So throughout the afternoon he worked from The Sunset Room, reviewing the contract he hadn't had a chance to look over last night. By six o'clock he was rubbing his tired eyes and moving from the table and chair he'd pulled close to the window, creating a makeshift office, standing to stretch. The chair wasn't as comfortable as the one he had in his real office and absently he wondered why he hadn't asked Lauren to replace it. Possibly that was because he never worked from the club, never spent more than a couple hours here at a time.

He hadn't really considered that point until this very moment. It was strange and then again, he supposed it wasn't. Jack was used to getting what he wanted. Nothing about the situation he now found himself in would change that.

Today had definitely been different, just as he suspected tonight would be. There was no question that he wanted Tara Sullivan, and subsequently none that he would eventually have her. He'd been on his way to accomplishing that goal last night, in the backseat of a car, no less. Jack did not do women in the backseat of a car. He did them in this room and this room only, he thought grimly, turning around and heading back to the bedroom. A quick glance around showed a different room than it had been the last time he was here, with Adonna.

The bed was now on the opposite wall, facing the windows, still a king size but now sitting on a marble platform, draped in a charcoal gray comforter with a number of pillows in more gray, white and a muted green tone. Above the bed were mirrors so that as he stood at the end of the bed, he looked directly at himself and saw what he'd always seen—a male, 6' 4½" tall, 210 lbs., suit pants, dress shirt, tie slightly askew, and tired eyes. Always tired eyes from too much reading, too much time spent in his drab colored office and not enough time on a secluded beach, relaxing, enjoying the spoils of his hard work. That's what his primary care doctor would say. With a shake of his head, Jack headed into the bathroom to take a quick shower.

He'd just finished fastening his belt when the cocktails had arrived. Not 10 minutes later, the soft buzz of the doorbell sounded again.

She was here.

Jack walked slowly, deciding he did not want to rush any part of this evening. He paused when touching the doorknob at the quickened beat of his heart. He was anticipating seeing her. It was a strange and new feeling, but as he opened the door, he welcomed it and her.

She looked stunning in a black dress that wrapped around every curve of her body, cupping her high breasts, gripping her rounded hips. Her hair was up once more, this time the bun on the right side of her head, giving her a different, sexier look. Her eyes were heavily made up tonight, so that they appeared darker, more exotic, her lips coated in a glossy red hue. And when she spoke, even her voice sounded smokier. It sounded as it had that night in New York.

"Hello, Tara. Come in," he told her, his mind churning with even more questions.

"I tried not to be late," he heard her saying as he was closing the door.

"Nonsense. Mercer will always get you where you need to be on time."

"I'm thinking of buying a car, maybe a hybrid," she said, her back still to him as she moved further into the living area. She seemed a bit nervous, chatting more than she usually did. Not that he didn't like the sound of her voice, or that he didn't want to hear more about her. He just wondered.

"I can make sure you get wherever you need to be. A car and driver can be at your beck and call."

She swung around to face him then.

"No. No, that's not necessary. I can drive myself," she insisted.

By that time he was close enough to her that he reached down, taking her purse from her hand and sitting it behind her on the new deep cushioned couch.

"I want to take care of you, Tara," Jack admitted. "Whatever you need, I will make sure you have."

"There's no need for that. You don't know me that well and—"

He was already dipping his head, placing a quick kiss on her soft lips to silence her. "After tonight, Tara, I will know you better than anyone ever has."

Jack thought he felt her stiffen at those words, but then she kissed him. Another quick, almost chaste kiss, except for the lightning bolts of heat that soared through him at the contact. The questions dissipated and he wrapped his arms around her waist. "I really enjoy kissing you."

"I enjoy kissing you, too," she told him.

"Good. Then we're going to enjoy each other thoroughly tonight. But first we'll have a drink. Have a seat."

"Just wine for me," she said when he'd moved away from her.

"I remember, Lotus Vineyard Cabernet Sauvignon," he stated, opening the new bottle and pouring her a glass.

After fixing himself a glass as well, Jack returned to the couch, taking a seat beside Tara and offering her the drink. She took it, giving him a small smile in return. He really liked her smiles, liked how they appeared to be only for him. Actually, he wanted them to be only for him, just as he wanted her all to himself.

"This is a really nice room," she said after taking a sip.

"How many of these rooms have you seen at The Corporation?"

She looked surprised at the question, or maybe it had been his tone. He'd felt slight agitation at her compliment of the room and the question had instantly popped into his head.

"I've only been here once," was her reply.

"And you did not stay. Why?"

She took a deep breath, released it, and stared down at her glass. "I was being a coward. But that's not who I am," she insisted, looking over at him then. "I know what I want and what I like. What I need."

Jack emptied his glass and reached over to the end table to put it down. He took Tara's glass and lifted her hands in his. "Tell me what you want, Tara. Whatever it is, I am here to give it to you."

This was not Jack's normal way of operating. In this room, at all times prior to this very moment, it had been about him, about his pleasure, his desires. Tonight, as he'd realized earlier, was unlike any other. It wasn't only the décor and the woman here with him. Jack was different, and he wasn't ready to explore why. All he knew was how he wanted tonight to end, with Tara naked and satisfied in his arms.

"I want to watch," she said, and then seemed to regret it as she closed her lips tightly. "I mean I want it...my life...everything to be different."

"I didn't know it until I saw you again, but I want the same thing," Jack readily admitted. "I want to show you how it can be different for both of us. Will you trust me to do that?"

Tara hesitated, her wide eyes surveying him, attempting to look deep enough to find any inkling of dishonesty. She was afraid of what tonight might actually bring, but strong enough to sit here and admit to an extent that this was where she needed to be. He admired the strength and determination she seemed to possess.

"Yes," was her eventual and quiet reply.

"Come with me," he said, standing and extending his hand to her.

Again, she hesitated.

"I will not hurt you, Tara. I want you to trust me, to trust what you are feeling and what you say you want."

She swallowed, nodding her head before taking his hand and standing. "I will," she replied confidently.

Keeping her hand in his, Jack walked them back to the bedroom. Originally, he'd planned to talk to her more, to see if she would mention New York and their first meeting or tell her anything about her past that Trent didn't seem to think existed. But there was something else at work here tonight, a force between the two of them that was stronger than any plan he'd thought he had, any reservations she fought to overcome.

He stopped in front of the bed, releasing her hand, and was just about to face her when he heard her sharp intake of breath and managed to catch her in his arms just as her knees buckled and she began to sink to the floor.

Tara's heart raced. Sweat pricked the base of her neck and her vision blurred.

Her vision had been perfectly clear the moment she entered that room and looked at the bed and then up...to the mirrors. A world of hurt and disgust and fear poured through the five second glance into herself.

She'd blinked but could still see Jana's face staring back at her. Jana's charcoal eyes, her plump red lips, her sophisticated and sexy hairstyle, her black dress and her smile. That's what sent the spear of pain through her chest, because Jana's smile had quickly been replaced by trickling blood, from the knife wound to the side of her head. Jana's mouth opened and there was that silent scream, that plea for help that Tara had not been able to oblige.

Now every part of her was shaking, her eyes closed so tightly she feared they may never open again. And there was warmth. Oh god, she was so damned hot. She felt like she couldn't take a deep inhalation because the space was so stuffy, so confined. She wanted to break free, to run, to scream, to leave her room where she had watched and burst into that house to help Jana, to save Jana.

"Tell me what you're afraid of Tara. What happened to you?"

His voice was right at her ear, amplified by the proximity, more warmth pouring over her. It wasn't Melvin's voice? She hadn't heard him that night? It was someone else, but she'd been alone. Nobody had been there with her while she watched. She was always alone at those times, preferred it that way.

"Tell me what's wrong so I can fix it," he continued.

His arms were tight around her, like a cocoon, surrounding her with heat and safety, something she'd never felt before. They were sitting now, where, she had no idea, but she didn't feel the room swaying around her any longer, didn't think she was going to smash her face on the floor when she fell.

"You can't fix it," she whimpered. "Nobody can."

"I can and I will," he pledged. "Just tell me what it is so I can make it better."

Tara had no idea how long she sat there in his embrace, waiting until her heart rate was steady. Her hands stopped trembling and her eyes fluttered with the urge to open, to see once again.

"Live for the moment," she said, even though she had no idea why. And actually, it hadn't even sounded like her voice.

But then her eyes opened and she looked up into his face, his handsome and serious face. She lifted a hand to lay along his cheek, to assure herself that he was real and not an object visible through her high-powered lens.

"I want you to touch me now. To please me," she told him.

For a brief second he looked as if he would choose to ask her another question instead. She prayed he would not, even though questions weren't the problem—the answers were.

"Wait here," he told her, his voice gruff, commanding. "Do not turn around, just stand right here."

Tara had no idea why, but she nodded, keeping her back straight and her gaze forward as he walked out of the room. Across from the bed were windows, floor-to-ceiling, just as they had been on the lower floors of The Corporation. A tall metal statue stood to one side. She was entranced by the smooth curves and lines, unable to take her gaze away from it until finally she realized why. It was a sculpture of a man and woman, bodies intertwined as if in the throes of ecstasy.

"The artist is amazing," Jackson said when he returned to the room. "His name is Lorenzo Bennett and I met him through a mutual friend."

She hadn't heard him approach, so she was slightly startled. He was moving as he continued to talk, going to a table she guessed, at the head of the bed, setting his glass down with a clink.

"I send him my thoughts and about six to eight months later he ships the sculpture. There are more at my condo."

"You don't live here?"

"No," he said, coming to stand in front of her. "I do not live here."

Tara nodded. She'd wanted to continue staring at the sculpture, but from the moment he returned to the room, she'd watched him instead. She was absorbed by his movements, the confidence and strength he exuded, and found herself drawing from him, taking everything he offered in something as inconsequential as walking.

"This is just the place you come to have sex," she stated, not sure how it would make her feel should his answer be "yes."

He knelt down in front of her, his hands cupping each of her knees, his eyes locking on hers.

"The Corporation is a club where any and all sexual fantasies come to life. It's a place where people come to lose all their inhibitions and to freely find the pleasure they crave."

He sounded like a commercial, a very convincing, sexy as hell commercial. She inhaled deeply, letting the aroma of his cologne seep through her entire body. Then she lifted a hand, her fingers shaking slightly as she touched his cheek. There was the smoothness of skin just before his light beard began and then the texture changed, still pleasing as the straight hair rasped along the inside of her hand.

"I know about cravings," she admitted. "I've had them all my life."

"And what have you done about those cravings, Tara? How have you found your pleasure?"

She'd admitted this to only one other man, and that had been for the purposes of putting a killer behind bars. Never had she told someone as a prelude to sex, or as an admission to what she'd like them to do for her. It was a weird feeling and yet, when her mouth opened, the words simply slipped free.

"I used to watch others," she told him.

When she opened her mouth to continue but instead paused, Jackson touched a finger to her chin, lifting her head so that their gazes held once more.

"You can trust me, Tara. Trust me with every fantasy, every longing, every need you have. I will take care of you, I promise."

He promised, the words dancing in her head. Nobody had ever promised her anything.

"I watched them hold hands at first, wondering how such an innocent touch could be so intimate. Then I watched them kiss and needed more."

"You needed to see their bodies connect, the rise and culmination of their pleasure," he continued. "And how did that make you feel when you saw it?"

The finger than had been running along the line of her jaw briefly touched her lips before she spoke.

"It made me feel good," she said in a voice so low she barely heard it.

"But not complete," he told her, letting that finger trace a line down the side of her neck, down further to whisper softly over her cleavage.

She bit her bottom lip, unable to answer.

"Stand up," he said suddenly, coming to his feet and holding a hand out to her.

Of course she hesitated, but as his hand hovered in front of her she eventually reached for it, putting hers inside and loving the warmth of his as it closed around her. She stood, her breasts pressing against his chest, her head tilting back so she could see his face.

"Kiss me, Tara."

She almost screamed "gladly," but instead wrapped her arms around his neck and, when he'd lowered his face to hers, she tilted slightly, letting her lips touch his. It was a soft contact at first, an exploration, even though she knew the explosiveness of their kiss already. Gently she let her tongue stroke over his lips until his met hers in a warm exchange. And then she plundered. She hugged him close to her, drinking of all the intimate goodness that kissing Jackson Carrington seemed to provide. He wrapped his arms around her, pulling her tight against him, his hands slipping down to cup her bottom.

As soft and endearing as the kiss had started out to be, it quickly moved to a hungry exchange, wherein both parties seemed to request more, to need the next step.

When her mind was full of what that next step might be, and when she felt like her body would be the first to give in, he broke the kiss.

Jackson pulled back from her, untwining her arms from his neck and placing them at her side.

"Trust me," he said while looking deeply into her eyes. "Trust me, Tara."

His hands went to her shoulders then and he turned her slowly until her ass was cradled against his thick erection and they were both facing the mirrors.

"Do you like to watch me, Tara?"

She knew the mirrors were there, but she had kept her gaze down as he spoke. Then he reached a hand around and touched her chin without applying any pressure.

"I would love for you to watch what I do to you," he continued. "That's why I had those mirrors installed earlier today. From now on I want you to watch me and only me."

Tara swallowed, but she did not look up. Not until he cupped her breast with one hand, and the finger at her chin pushed her head upward. She'd blinked one long time, afraid of who she would see looking back at her, what memories would slap her painfully if she dared look. But her eyes would not remain closed, as if even they wanted some relief to the standoff taking place inside her.

Tara let go a ragged breath when she could finally see. His fingers squeezed around her breast while she felt the heat spreading through her at that same moment. His other hand touched her face gently, sliding across her jaw to her ear and then to her hair, where he pulled the bun free in a matter of seconds.

Her heart pattered quickly, her eyes transfixed on that mirror, on the sight before her.

"I want to see all of you," Jackson told her.

Tara didn't respond. She didn't feel she had to.

His hands moved over her expertly, undoing the clasps of the dress and letting it fall to the floor as if he'd been the one to put it on her as well. She'd worn black underwear, a lacy wisp of fabric over her neatly shaved vagina and a matching bra that was so transparent her darkened nipple was visible through the mirror. But when his hands, a lighter tone than her complexion, touched the black lace, it sent shivers through her. She felt warm all over, and needy as hell.

With both hands, he cupped her breasts now, lifting them up, pushing them together, and kneading them in a way that had her thighs shivering.

"See how delicious you look," he told her while one hand slid down her torso, over her navel, beneath the rim of her thong.

His entire palm flattened over the V between her legs and Tara gasped.

"Hold on to me," he demanded. "Don't let me go and don't close your eyes."

She did as she was told, lifting both arms up and back so that her fingers were now gripping his shirt. Her legs had parted involuntarily as she moved so that now she was spread out for him.

"I'm going to make you come," he announced.

She gasped.

"Yes. I will be the first besides yourself to bring you release."

She began shaking her head.

"Please do not deny me this pleasure, Tara. Do not deny us."

He'd said please as if it were an actual plea, as if maybe if she did deny them he would end up as broken and unfixable as she. But there was strength in his words as well. He knew she would not say no. He knew his touch was better than anything she'd ever felt before, that watching him touch her was better than any scene she'd ever viewed.

She lay her head back against his chest, her tongue snaking out to swipe her bottom lip. "Yes, please," she whispered.

His finger slipped through the plump folds of her pussy, already slick with desire. He touched her clit and she moaned softly, pushed back further until that finger was sucked instantaneously into her waiting heat. Her walls clenched around him, eager for the attention, anxious for the release.

"Wider," he told her, his voice only slightly strained. "Open wider."

She did and another finger pressed deep inside her. Her thighs shivered and she undulated her hips, more than ready for him to start pumping, to start pressing against her spot, bringing forth the surge of pleasure.

"Don't."

One word. One direction and she stilled completely.

"I will take care of you."

And he did. In the next moment his fingers moved masterfully inside her, pulling in and out, milking her of all the essence she had stored inside. The palm of his hand rubbed enticingly over her clit, making breathing an almost impossibility. Faster and faster he pumped inside of her until keeping still had her biting down on her lip so hard she thought it would bleed.

"Come for me, sweetness," he whispered, his lips right up against her ear. "Come for me, now. All of you in my hand, right now. Come!"

Her entire body shivered, her vision blurry through the slits of her eyes as she watched herself going limp in his arms. His hand was buried deep inside her pussy. The other one had slipped beneath the material of the bra to squeeze her nipple. He licked her ear after speaking, and then looked at her through the mirror.

"Come, Tara. Watch yourself come for only me," he pushed her.

And she did. She watched her legs shake, her chest heave and a part of the world she knew shatter into a million tiny bright pieces. It was brilliant and beautiful and arousing and everything. Just everything.

And then there was more.

Jack's heartbeat thundered in his ears as he reluctantly pulled his hand from the splendid warmth of her pussy. Stepping from behind her, he reached into his back pocket for the pieces of black satin he'd retrieved when he'd left the room. She still looked dazed, the euphoria of her release wrapped firmly around her.

He picked her up, holding her close as her head lulled against his shoulder. A part of him wanted to cuddle her just this way, to simply lay on this bed and hold her close. Another part needed to claim, to control, to ensure that tonight would only be the beginning.

As he lifted her arm to the bed post, she turned to look at him, her mouth poised to question.

He touched a finger to her lips. "Trust me," was his simple order.

She relaxed only minutely as he tied her wrist to the post and then repeated the action with the other. Spreading her legs apart, he tied her ankles to the end of the bed and then stood once again at the bottom, looking down at her.

"Keep your eyes on me, Tara. Watch me take you once more."

She blinked, but she couldn't keep her eyes closed. He loved that look she had when she was watching. It was a hooded look that made her expressive eyes seem more exotic. Her lips trembled and her body softened. Damn, her body had softened and moistened and almost sent him right over the edge with desire. He never realized how much he liked to be watched until it was Tara's gaze arousing him.

He unbuttoned his shirt, taking it off slowly, watching for any sign that she was enjoying what she saw. It came seconds later when his chest was bare and she gasped. Jack had been naked in front of women before, but never really paid a lot of attention to whether or not they enjoyed the sight. Tonight, he was overwhelmed with the pleasure he saw in her eyes and the desire to give her his very best.

He removed his shoes and his pants, letting his boxer briefs stay on just a moment longer.

"How much more do you want, Tara? What else can I give you tonight?"

He had no idea why he'd asked. It wasn't his forte. He announced what he wanted and he received it, and then the interlude was finished. That was the way Jackson Carrington worked in business and pleasure. Until tonight.

"Everything," had been her quick reply. "I want everything."

With his gaze locked on hers, he slid his boxers down his thighs, his hard length jutting forward, the plan to give her everything already settling in his mind.

Jack walked around to the side of the bed, first pulling open the top drawer and returning with a condom that seconds later he had sheathing his length. Next, he picked up the fresh glass of vodka and cranberry he'd set there moments earlier. Moving to the bed he touched the glass to her lips, using his other hand to hold her head so she could sip. She gulped instead and he smiled.

"I'm thirsty too," he told her when she finished, and he moved the glass to his lips next.

She watched him swallow, watched his fingers slip inside the glass and pull out the ice cube, then rubbing it along the line of her lips. Her mouth opened slightly, letting the moisture inside, some drops rolling down her chin. He popped the ice into his mouth then, chewing it slowly as she watched his lips move.

Once more his finger went into the glass and then moved over her breasts, where he let drops of the light pink liquid fall onto her mounds. She shivered, her breasts moving with the motion, and Jack moved closer, kneeling on the bed beside her now. He dripped more onto her chest, this time leaning forward to cover one drenched nipple with his mouth, sucking until it was once again dry. He drew the next nipple into his mouth, loving the feel of the turgid tip against his tongue alongside the smooth tang of the vodka.

Her breath was coming in quick pants, her chest rising up, falling down. When he dripped more between the center of her breasts, he smiled as the droplets found their way down her torso and raced to lick each one before it fell to the bed. Her navel, he used as a cup, pouring, then drinking, pouring and then drinking some more. All the while she squirmed beneath him, making his body harder, more ready for her with each second.

But Jack wasn't finished. There was more of her he wanted to taste. At this point he was driven by an intense need that he'd never encountered before. Seeing her sweet pussy bared to him would never be enough. He would feel those thick vulva lips in his mouth and taste her sweet explosion before the night was over.

His glass was almost empty when he tilted it once more, angling the downpour directly over her mound. Again the lines of liquid raced to an end and he threw the glass to the side, quickly ducking his head and slurping every ounce. She bucked beneath him and he put his hands on her thighs to keep her still while his tongue licked and lapped every drop. When he was sure the remnants of the drink were gone from the smoothness of her skin, Jack's hands moved to cup her ass cheeks, lifting her like a delectable dessert to his face before diving in.

She was soft and pliant, sweet and irresistible. His arms even shook as he continued trying to hold her in place, until it was just too much for him to continue, too much torture for him to bare. Hurriedly he untied her legs, lifting them onto his shoulders as he angled himself over her.

He was about to instruct her to watch but it was pointless. Her hot and aroused gaze was already fixated on him. With a free hand, he stroked his latex covered length and moved closer to her entrance.

"All you have to do is tell me to stop," he told her, knowing it would be like walking over fire to do what she asked. "At any time, Tara, just tell me to stop."

She shook her head. "I want it all. Now," she breathed. "Now!"

Tara was gloriously tight and blissfully wet. The head of his cock pressed into her with seeming ease, the rest of his length squeezing past the barrier as he clenched his teeth to keep from exploding at that very moment. She rocked against him, opening for him, taking him in, all while moaning ever so softly.

He leaned forward instinctively, wanting to swallow those soft moans as they came, stroking inside her deeper and deeper still. With a start he realized he wanted to feel her hands on him, wanted her to touch him the way he was touching her, to hopefully feel the sensation of falling as he did. Reaching up, he pulled the bindings at her arms free. She was fast, eager, and probably as hungry for this connection as he was. In seconds her arms were wrapping around him, her blunt nails digging into the bare skin of his shoulders as she voraciously met each of his thrusts.

Jack wanted to say something to her, wanted to tell her how perfect she was, how absolutely divine being inside of her had turned out to be. But he didn't. He couldn't. Instead, he rolled onto his side, bringing her with him, keeping his length buried deep inside her wetness. He locked his hand behind one thigh, lifting it high up to his hip and thrust deeper into her core. Her hands cupped his face and his body trembled.

"Thank you," she whispered and kissed his lips. "Thank you."

Jack was in a frenzy now, feeling heat, desire, longing and something unexplainable, something that clenched inside his chest so tight he thought he might be having some type of coronary episode. He kissed her fervently, moving his hips with a rhythm that had the sound of their joining echoing throughout the room. She moaned into his mouth and his other hand sank into the strands of her hair, tugging slightly. She bit his lip when she came, licking over the spot just seconds before he exploded deep inside her.

How long they lay there, Jack had no idea. Bodies intertwined like the statue near his window, their breaths steadying eventually. When she shivered in his arms, Jack moved them so that they could be under the blankets. He took a second to dispose of the condom and then joined her again, pulling her close, wrapping himself around her like a cocoon, deciding then and there that he had no intention of ever letting her go.

CHAPTER NINE

"Stay with me," he'd said some time during the night.

And she'd stayed.

It had been a night of many firsts—first time orgasm from a man, first time multiple orgasm, first time enjoying sex with a man, first time watching herself have sex with a man.

It was morning now and Tara had no clue what the protocol was. Should she creep out of his bed and leave before he awoke? Maybe she should cook breakfast? Unfortunately, she was almost positive there was no kitchen in this suite. This wasn't Jackson's home. It was his love nest, or whatever he called it. Laying on her side with his arm draped over her, his hand splayed over her stomach, she wondered if she should feel a certain way about that.

No, she decided. She hadn't come here last night in search of a relationship or any emotional entanglement. She'd come as a step forward, as a milestone in this new life she'd been given. And now it was time to leave.

"I want to spend the weekend with you."

Tara hadn't thought he was awake, so the sound of his voice startled her. She jumped and he hugged her closer, nuzzling his face into her neck.

"Sorry," he said, his voice still husky with sleep. "I should have said good morning first."

"Why do you want to spend the weekend with me?" she asked, her gaze focused on the lamp on the nightstand.

"I want to find out what else you like besides red wine," he told her, pushing her hair aside and kissing the base of her neck. "I want to watch you eat another steak salad." Another kiss, this time a little farther down the line of her spine.

"I want to talk about your business and your hopes for the future." The next kiss included more tongue and was near the center of her back, his hand creeping around to cup her breast. "I want to be with you every moment that I can," he finished, his tongue tracing a heated path all the way down to the base of her back.

He moved to one side of her rounded ass, kissing one cheek and then the other before asking, "Is that a problem?"

She didn't know what to say. Her mind had originally been focused on the questions he was asking, but quickly became diverted by the warmth of his mouth on her skin and the instantaneous reaction her body had to his touch. Before she could speak, he was turning her so that she was flat on her stomach and he was moving between her spread legs.

"Look up, sweetness," he instructed her. "Look up and watch me pleasure you again."

Tara pressed down on the pillow, lifting her chin so that she could see into the mirrors that lined the wall behind the bed. Sunlight trickled in through the motorized blinds, and Jackson's silhouette was surrounded by a golden glow. He pushed her slightly upward so that she was on her knees with her torso still flat on the bed. Then his dark head lowered and his tongue touched her moist lips.

She gasped, watching as her mouth slightly opened, eyes wide. Her bottom was in the air, his lighter toned hands clenching each cheek, spreading her wide. He licked her clit, tugged the sensitive nub into his mouth and suckled. Her fingers gripped the pillow case tightly, her teeth biting down on her lower lip. His tongue slipped further back, dipping inside her center, fucking her so sweetly. Her thighs shook, her lids closing heavily, and then lifting again slowly as if she were on some type of drug. Back further still, his tongue explored until he was at her rear.

Tara moaned then, wanting desperately to watch, helpless against the onslaught of pleasure whipping intensely through her body. She closed her eyes and shivered, feeling the waves of release pressing down on her quickly, torrentially. In the next instant, Jackson moved to the nightstand, ripping open the package to another condom, smoothing it over his heavy, thick length.

When he was between her legs again, his hands planted on her hips, his gaze commanding hers through the mirror, he repeated his earlier question, "Is there a problem with that?"

The head of his cock pressed slowly against her entrance and Tara squirmed with anticipation, remnants of her recent release dripping down her thighs. "No," she whispered. "No problem, at all. Please, Jackson," she whimpered, hating and loving the sound all at once. "Please."

"Whatever you want," he told her, his hands rubbing over her ass. "Whatever you need."

"I need this," she stuttered, wiggling her ass back against his dick, aching for him to thrust long and deep. "Yes, I need this."

"I know what you need, sweetness. Trust me, I know."

Once more he separated her cheeks, this time dragging his dick back toward her rear and then down to her opening, spreading her essence throughout until the slick sound had her gasping.

"Now! Please!" she yelled.

And before she could inhale again, he thrust so deep inside her she felt like they were conjoined. Her head fell into the pillow then, her heart thumping so fast she was sure he could hear it too. She circled her hips, trying to get more of him inside, needing to feel him everywhere at once.

"Keep still," he ordered, his voice louder than her heartbeat. "Let me take care of you."

She stilled immediately at the sound of his voice, having heard that tone a few times throughout the night. If she did what he said, he gave her everything he promised and then some. She'd never thought there would be such give and take, never imagined it possible and never dreamed she would be on the receiving end. And while she had no idea how long this affair would last, she was determined to enjoy every second of it.

So Tara didn't move. She kept her knees planted firmly on that bed, lifted her head so she could watch through the mirrors and waited for the pleasure once more. She waited for Jackson to give her everything he'd promised her.

And damn, did he.

With quick strokes he pulled out and dove deep inside her, over and over until she was panting, her mind free of worries, of fears or recriminations and full of Jackson Carrington.

$\sim$

"I haven't heard from her since that first call," Jerald told Jack over the phone, the next day.

Jack was at his office, hoping to finalize the deal tonight so he'd have the entire weekend free to be with Tara.

"She's definitely back in L.A. I had lunch with her father yesterday," Jack informed him.

"Really? Since when do you go to lunch with anyone that's not on your business radar?"

"Since his nutcase of a daughter tried threatening my family," was Jack's instant response. "Winston doesn't know where she's been these past years. Apparently she's kept in touch but hasn't been, in his words, 'pestering him for money,' so he's been content just to receive a phone call every few weeks."

"It's a damn shame when her own father doesn't miss her."

"No, what's a shame is that she's trying this now, of all times." Jack sat back in his chair, rubbing a finger over his chin as he thought about the situation. "She must have heard about the RGA deal."

"Come on, Jack, you know the last thing Soleil would do is read a newspaper, and a business section no less. How would she even now about the deal?"

"Remember last month when Mom and Dad went to Miami? Dad was being interviewed for the documentary on that cable network. He talked about Carrington Enterprises and what was on the horizon for us."

"I still don't see Soleil giving a damn what we're doing on the business front."

Jack persisted. "She would if this is about money."

"But is it about money?" Jerald asked. "Because the more I replay the conversation with her, the smug way in which she said all the Carrington men would pay, I got the impression she was acting out a much more personal vendetta."

"Then she's definitely barking up the wrong tree because none of us ever slept with her crazy ass. There's nothing she can have on us." Jack let that sentence replay in his mind long after he hung up with Jerald.

There was something that could be used against his family, something that only he knew about and that was in his complete control to stop. But there was no way Soleil Ducovney could know about his ownership in the club. She wasn't a member. He was sure of that. Or he would be after he made a call to have the complete member list emailed to him ASAP.

At almost five o'clock he called out to his assistant, DeMarco. "Tell Mercer I'll be ready in 20 minutes. And call ahead to the cabin to make sure everything is ready. I don't want any issues when I get there."

Jack hung up with DeMarco and called Trent Donovan. He had more questions and needed the investigator to come up with the answers.

The first thing Tara noticed the next morning when she entered her house was the quiet.

It was too quiet.

"Vicious," she called to her puppy, who should have been running to meet her at the door. "Here, girl. I'm home," she continued.

Silence.

She'd already stepped out of the heels she'd worn out last night and now carried them and her purse up the stairs as she went in search of her dog.

"Vicious, come on out girl," she yelled when she was at the top of the steps.

But there was still no reply. No barking, no running to her and around her anxiously, waiting to be scooped up into her arms. A slither of panic immerged at the thought.

"Vicious," she was yelling once more, going through each of the three rooms and the bathroom on the top floor.

She checked beneath her bed, behind the dresser where Vicious liked to play, in the closets and down to the end of the hall where there was a picture window that Vicious would sometimes climb up and in to look outside. Nothing.

Tara ran down the steps calling to her dog again, trying desperately not to become hysterical. Vicious was all she had left. Tara needed her dog. She'd been with her for so long. She loved her unconditionally. It didn't matter that she was starting over, becoming a new woman. She needed that small piece of the past, that constant that had seen her through so much.

"Vicious!" she yelled, her head going from side to side, looking throughout the house.

It was at that moment that she smelled it. It stank like something rotten, something gross and she wondered why she hadn't smelled it when first entering the house. Her stomach churned, her hands shaking as she followed the stench, moving back through the house to the kitchen. Steam filled the air, billowing up in thick puffs coming from the stove.

"What the hell?" she murmured as she moved closer.

There was a huge stainless steel crab pot on her stove, with something boiling inside. Something…not someone or some dog…please not…

She moved slowly, every step making her that much more nauseous, her brow beginning to sweat. At her sides her hands shook even as she reached over to snag one of the potholders hanging from clips on the cabinet door.

"No, no," she was saying now, convincing herself. "No. No. No."

With the potholder secure on her hand, she extended her arm to the top that was now bubbling over. Dark pink water sloshed onto her white stove and onto the tiled floor, the aroma causing an instant gagging sound as she stood directly over the pot.

"No," she whispered once more as she touched the top and lifted it slowly.

The scream that erupted should have shattered every window in the place. Tara dropped the top onto the stove and immediately backed away, the heel of her hand pressed into her mouth to stifle any more sound.

At that same moment there was a knock at her door and she jumped, wanting to yell again but biting into her hand instead. At the pain, she yanked her hand away and took a breath.

The knocking was persistent. Probably someone had heard her screaming. She didn't want to see anyone, didn't want to explain what she couldn't understand herself. Someone had obviously been in her house. With that thought, she moved quickly to yank open one of the drawers, grabbing the first knife she could find before heading to the door. If there was a killer on the other side, they were about to meet their match—or at least a very angry opponent, which might prove even more lethal.

On the fifth knock, Tara yanked open the door and received another fright.

"Having a dog's a responsibility. If you're gonna stay out all night, get a dogsitter, or, how about this? Make sure you get home early enough to take your dog out and feed it," Russ said with a scowl, thrusting a furry white ball in front of her face.

"Vicious," she sighed, dropping the knife to the floor and taking her puppy from Russ's big meaty hands. "Oh my god, I was so scared. So scared you were..." she whispered, nuzzling her dog close to her chin, receiving with relish her licks of excitement along her face.

Then it hit her, and she looked up frowning. "If you're here, then what's that?" She looked towards the stove, and then to Russ—who had apparently been inside her house while she was gone, again. "What did you do and why the hell do you keep breaking into my house?"

Russ had already moved past her, his hulking form now standing over the stove, blocking the boiling pot from her view. He hadn't responded to her but was reaching one tattooed arm up to turn off the flame.

"Goddammit!" he finally exclaimed.

"What is it?" she asked taking a step closer. "What did you do?"

Russ whirled around so fast he was in her face before she could form another question. Vicious barked at him, her little teeth bared in defense, and Tara held onto her tightly.

"I didn't do anything! But you! Who stays out all night when they know a killer's looking for them? Are you really that fuckin' horny that you just couldn't stay your ass in this house so I could keep an eye on things. Don't you get that your life is still in danger?" he yelled at her, veins building at his temple, dark eyes blaring with rage.

She'd never seen him look like this before, never felt this complete and utter abhorrence from anyone in her life. In that moment, fear greater than any she'd felt in this past year skated down her spine and she took a step back.

"I'm calling Emilio," she said tightly.

"You do that!" Russ spat. "I'll search the rest of this place to see how they got in."

He'd said they, but Tara wondered.

Russ was the only one here now. Just as he'd been the only one to see that sedan circling around her house.

Half an hour later, Emilio was walking into her dining room where she sat at the small round table, staring down at the lattice placemats she'd purchased online a couple of weeks ago. Vicious sat in her lap.

"They came in through the basement. There's some partial prints on the door. I've called for some backup to come and take a look," he said while pulling out a chair and sitting down beside her.

"Big Mel is in Allenwood. He's under maximum security. I've had Penelli's apartment in the city and his house in the Hamptons under surveillance since Russ reported seeing that sedan. So far we haven't seen any of his backup hit men paying him a visit."

"You said all I had to do was testify and this would be over. You said I'd have a new life and I could do what I wanted to do with it." She looked up at him then. "You lied."

As if today couldn't get any stranger in her eyes, Tara was startled yet again when Emilio's blue eyes actually looked sorrowful and when his hand came up to cup her cheek.

"I'm sorry," he said. "I never wanted to see that look of fear in your eyes again."

His voice was so calm, so filled with emotion, she didn't know how to immediately respond. Emilio had taken more time with her than any of the other marshals. He'd given her more leeway, paid more attention to the requests she'd made, or was the one to simply sit and talk to her more than the others. Yet, he'd done all that and still managed to frown at knowing her sexual preferences.

The preferences that had taken her in an entirely different direction last night. Jackson, she thought with a start. He was sending his car to pick her up at seven tonight so they could go away for the weekend. How would he react to seeing Emilio and the rest of the marshals here? He would ask questions. Too many questions, including one she knew she did not want to answer.

"Can you find out who is doing this?" she asked Emilio. "Can you stop them?"

He nodded, dropping his hand from her face. "It's my job to protect you."

"Maybe it's time I started protecting myself," she told him. "I will not stay locked in this house, Emilio. I gave up everything I knew to get justice for Jana. I deserve this new life. I deserve to live!"

"Yes. You do," he told her. "And I'm going to make sure you get to live it. I can put in a request to have a marshal re-assigned to you 24-7. With these new developments, that shouldn't be a problem."

"Russ seems to be here all the time," she told him. "But he's not assigned to be is he?"

Emilio sat back in the chair, letting his palms rest on his knees. "No. He's not officially assigned."

"So why does he keep breaking into my house? Why is he always the one to see something, or notice something? Have you thought about that?" She was asking these questions, but she'd only thought of them herself in the last hour she'd been home. Russell Samuels was a U.S. Marshal. He was not a hired killer. At least, she'd never thought of him as one before.

"I don't know those answers," Emilio told her. "But I've thought of the questions and I'm keeping an eye on that situation as well."

It was her turn to nod.

"The old me would have been frightened, not wanting to leave this house. And I would have been trusting," she said looking up at him. "But the new me," she added with a shake of her head. "Not so much."

She lifted Vicious into her arms and stood from the chair. With a voice as steady as she was feeling at this very moment, she told Emilio, "I'm going away for the weekend with a friend. Search the house, do whatever you have to do to find out who is still after me and catch the sonofabitch once and for all."

He stood immediately, touching a hand to her shoulder. "Wait a minute, Tara. You can't just go off someplace without adequate protection. And who is this friend? I thought you didn't know anyone here."

She looked down to where his hand rested on her shoulder—the same shoulder that Jackson had kissed and bit lightly as he'd rode her from behind this morning. The memory had her moving slightly so that Emilio's hand no longer touched her.

"As I said before, I have a life to lead. That means I'll meet people and I'll have connections and I'll grow into a stronger, more resilient person. That's what Jana would have wanted for me. That's what I want for myself."

"Tara, listen to me," he continued. "I can't protect you if I don't know where you are or who you're with. What if this new 'friend' is the one taunting you? Have you ever thought about that?" he asked pointedly. "It may not be such a coincidence that the moment you start going out that someone has gotten close enough to you to boil a damned rabbit on your stove."

The stench still lingered in the house, the memory of that steaming pot and the fear that it was Vicious inside had her chest tightening. But Tara wouldn't waver. She couldn't.

"If he is, I'll find out soon enough," she replied. "But I won't run and hide, not again."

"It's about self-preservation," he said as she'd begun to move out of the room.

"No, Emilio, it's about finding myself. And I'm not about to let some coward assed wannabe killer keep me from reaching for what I want. If he really wanted me dead, he knows where I live and obviously how to get into my house. Why hasn't he succeeded yet? For whatever reason, Penelli ordered Big Mel to kill Jana. And he did it without boiling rabbits or riding around in dark colored cars. So if this bastard is serious, then let him come and get me. Believe me, I'm tougher than I look."

With that, Tara left Emilio standing there speechless. She went upstairs to her room and closed her door. After a second of deep breathing, she sat Vicious to the floor and went about packing her bag for the weekend. When that was done, she booted up her computer and checked her due dates for contracted assignments and did some other administrative work. She didn't hear when the marshals left, didn't reply when Emilio sent a text to her phone.

She did, however, pull up a file she hadn't looked at in months. When the picture popped up onto the screen, she attempted unsuccessfully to blink back the tears. Tara stared into dark eyes with long lashes, high cheekbones and a smile that was like a punch in the gut every time. She whispered, as one tear dripped down her cheek, "Jana."

CHAPTER TEN

Tara had been standing on the balcony, staring out at the rolling waves for almost 20 minutes now. They'd arrived at Jack's cabin in Big Sur a little after midnight and had immediately gone to bed. In the morning she had been up and in the kitchen cooking breakfast before he'd awakened.

During the meal she'd asked questions about his family and his business as if she were a reporter, taking note of each answer like it was fitting a puzzle piece into place. He'd obliged her and had not demanded she reciprocate by telling him more of her past because there'd been a look in her eyes since he'd picked her up the night before. It was an unhappy, resigned look that he was certain he didn't like. What Jack was also certain of was that before this weekend ended, he would know exactly who Tara Sullivan was and why there were moments when fear and sadness seemed to engulf her all at once.

For now, however, with her dog sleeping soundly on a cushion by the patio door, Jack simply stood, watching her watch the water, and wondered how much pain he would cause by delving into her past.

He stepped out onto the deck, but remained a distance away from her. She didn't jump this time, as she had when he'd come into the kitchen behind her, or as he'd closed and locked the door behind them when they arrived last night. No, her shoulders seemed a little more relaxed this afternoon, her hair held loosely at the base of her neck by a colored band. The curves of her body were visible through the thin, mesh-like material top she wore over a pink and black bikini he'd purchased for her. Her bare feet added an innocence to an otherwise alluring look.

"If you had children, would you try to censor their life?" she asked without turning around.

Jack took a seat on one of the cushioned patio chairs.

"I don't believe in censorship," was his reply.

She'd been asking these types of questions all morning, framing them to his life, yet leaving just a hint of how close they were to her own.

"Do you want to have children, Tara?"

"I don't want to ruin anyone's life," was her immediate reply. "I don't want to be responsible for taking something away from another human being just because I believe it's the right thing to do."

"Is that what happened to you? Did someone take away a part of your life, and now you're angry about it?"

She turned then, slowly, letting her backside rest against the maple wood railing that wrapped around the entire side of the cabin.

"You said your parents had high expectations for you and your brothers. How did you deal with that? Did you ever think you couldn't meet their demands?" she asked him.

Jack thought about the question for a moment, wondering if she knew how close she was hitting to home.

"They wanted what was best for all three of us. But sometimes parents don't immediately understand that what they think is best, might not be. My younger brother, Jason, had to prove that he could be successful in his own business. That was a hard pill for my father to swallow, but he did, because he loves his son."

"You followed his footsteps, though. Every step of the way, right? You went to the same college as your father, graduated tops in your class, moved on to work in the family company and now you're running the show. Just as your father wanted? That must make you both proud."

No, Jack thought solemnly, it made him a coward. That thought did not sit well with him, and he gritted his teeth to keep from yelling out his response.

"I'm no saint, if that's what you're getting at," he told her.

She tilted her head to the side, this time contemplating him. "Why do you say that? Have I ever dubbed you a saint?"

"No. You haven't. But some do," he admitted without really knowing why.

Jack had always felt comfortable at the cabin. He'd purchased it two years ago, but had only managed to tear himself away from work three times to spend a few days here. And he'd always come alone. Bringing Tara here had been a spur of the moment decision, one he hadn't thought he needed to analyze. Watching her in the kitchen this morning and now standing here with a self-assured inquisitiveness made him see that she belonged here. Another factor he hadn't really considered.

"I'm not everything that I appear, Tara."

"You mean, your penchant for controlled sexual escapades is nobody's business but your own?"

One lovely brow arched while she spoke in a tone that was neither judgmental nor distasteful. It simply was, just like the sun was shining and the waves were rolling in.

"My family does not know that I own part of The Corporation. It's not something that they would understand, and it would be detrimental to the image that I and our company uphold."

And he'd never said that aloud to anyone in his entire life. Yet there was no bitterness now after the admission.

She pulled her arms back, letting her hands rest along the railing behind her. There was more on her mind, more questions or observations, he could tell. But there was also something else.

"Undress for me," she told him. "I want to watch you."

Tara wasn't sure he would do as she asked. Jackson liked to be in control, he liked to give the directives, and she had to admit she didn't mind following them. But just at this moment, as she'd stood looking at him with the red wood of the cabin surrounding him, the rich tall green trees in the background and the sound of the rushing waves of the ocean just feet away, she'd been aroused.

This feeling was new to her in that she'd always wanted to watch others having sex together. She knew that there were some who got off from watching the simplest things like someone cutting the grass, or jogging around the track. But for her it always had to be the sex, the sin she'd been warned against all her life. That was what got her off every time.

Until last night.

Until Jackson.

Last night she'd watched herself orgasm. She'd seen as well as felt the rush of desire explode inside her body. He'd cupped her breasts in his hands, squeezing until they were bursting through his fingers. Those same fingers had fucked her until she was crazy with need, wanting his dick inside her more than she wanted air. And when he'd given it to her, she'd soared, higher and higher until she thought she would simply float away.

"Take off that cover up," she heard him say, interrupting her pleasurable memories from last night.

She blinked and stared.

"I want to see the bathing suit."

He was sitting with his legs gaped open, his hands on either end of the chair, not moving a muscle. She'd told him she wanted to watch him and she should have known better. In this, he would always call the shots. She should have realized. Still, the tone of his voice, that gentle command struck a chord within her every time, sending a spike of pure lust straight to the center of her pussy as if hitting the bull's eye.

Reaching for the hem of the mesh cover-all, Tara pulled it up and over her head, letting it fall from her fingers to the planked porch. There was a soft breeze, a touch of the humidity that clung to the air smoothing over her bared skin. She inhaled deeply, loving the salted sea air as it wafted through her nostrils. Her tongue had just come out to stroke along her top and bottom lips when Jackson pulled his t-shirt up and over his head.

His chest was bare and she just barely avoided gasping. His strength was in everything from the way he walked to the sound of his voice. The moment he entered a room, he commanded attention and acquiescence, as if it were his birthright. The perfectly sculpted lines of his abs and bulge of his biceps only accentuated the obvious.

He sat still while she looked her fill, knowing she was looking and needing at the same time. Her fingers wiggled at her sides as memory of running them over his taut pectorals filled her mind. She hadn't tasted him, she thought with a start, her mouth instantly watering as she wondered if he would let her.

When his hands went to the drawstring of his linen lounge pants, she sucked in another huge gulp of air, releasing it slowly as he stood. He kicked the leather slippers he'd been wearing to the side and pushed the pants down to the floor, stepping out of them before moving to stand in front of the chair once more.

"Come here, Tara," he beckoned her.

She was walking before her name completely left his lips, anticipation a buzz throughout the air.

"Take them off."

She reached for the ban of his boxer briefs, pushing them over his tight ass, down his muscled thighs, tossing them to the side after he'd stepped out of them. When she would have stood again, he put a hand to her shoulder and told her, "Stay there and watch."

Heat swarmed at the spot where he'd touched, trickling throughout her body as she positioned herself on her knees, her face only inches away from his engorged sex.

"Watch," he stated again, softer this time, as the hand from her shoulder moved to grip his thick length.

Her gaze centered there, locking, and her breath came in quick shallow pants. The roped veins in his arms, going down to the backs of his hands, seemed to pulsate as he palmed his dick, pulling upward until the bulbous head looked like it would explode. He moved excruciatingly slow, all the way to the tip, where he let his thumb rub along the slit, back down to the base. His legs were slightly parted so that his sac was also visible, looking heavy and tight. Again her fingers itched to touch, her mouth, watering to taste.

When he began to move with a quicker rhythm, his hand against his own skin making a slapping sound, her breathing picked up, her mouth opened, air whooshing in and slipping out Her breasts felt heavy and swollen, her pussy drenched with desire. A pearl drop appeared at his slit and her entire body shivered. Tara looked up to see Jackson staring down intently at her.

"You want it?" he asked, a muscle in his jaw ticking as he spoke.

"Yes," she breathed in response.

"Take it," he told her. "Take it all, Tara."

She didn't wait to be told again. She couldn't. Her heart was beating so fast and so loud it was like a drum beat in her ears. Her need was so great she felt like she might actually pass out if she didn't touch him, taste him, have him in some way. She had no idea how she'd survived on just watching before, no clue as to what she would have done if he hadn't offered this to her.

So she took. She leaned in, tongue extended and touched the inviting tip of his gorgeous dick, letting the smooth, warm drop tickle her tongue. She stayed close, loving the mixture of his musky scent and the sea air as it mingled in her nose. Swallowing the drop was like taking a bite of decadent chocolate. One taste was not going to be enough.

"I said take it all," he told her in that voice again.

His hand was at the base of his cock, the thick length extended to her, its tip still wet from where she licked. Tara opened her mouth and took him inside. The tip was thicker than she'd imagined and her lips spread wider to accommodate him.

"More," Jackson prodded.

She opened wider, moved in closer over his length, feeling his heat slide inside her mouth, her eyes closing with the pleasure.

"Eyes on me, Tara. You wanted to watch, remember?"

Tara's eyes shot open because she did remember. She'd wanted to see him just like this, and now she was seeing and tasting. She was in heaven, a safer and more enjoyable place she'd never known.

So she watched him as she deep throated him, relaxing her throat muscles as the tip of his dick touched her throat. Closing her mouth over him she sucked gently at first, then hollowing her cheeks for more suction. Jackson did not issue another command. He did release his hold on his cock to thread his fingers into her hair, pulling it free.

She touched him then, using both hands to wrap her fingers around his length, stroking along his dick the same way he had while sucking him off. His thumbs rubbed along her cheekbones as he held her head steady, setting the pace of how much of him she would take and how much he would give. She was gasping for breath now, her mouth so wet she was dripping all over his cock and down onto her hands.

And he was perfectly quiet.

Until she touched his sac, letting her fingers roll over the tightness while she took him deeper into her mouth.

"Sweetness," he gasped. "Such fucking sweetness. Come for me, now."

At the sound of his voice, the hitch of pure pleasure in his tone, she came. Her thighs shivered as her orgasm ripped through her like a torrential storm.

"Ah, you wanted to come first, I see. Naughty girl," he said, wrapping her hair around his hands and pulling until her scalp tingled.

He pumped into her mouth then, slow, measured movements, building a rhythm that made his face go grim with concentration, his eyes like black orbs as he stared down at her. When he came he went still, the corner of his mouth lifting in a smile. "Take it all, Tara."

And she did. Breathing in his scent, swallowing his essence, breathing out, swallowing some more until he was finished. He pulled his length from her lips with a plopping sound and then lifted her up into his arms.

"I want you to come again, Tara. All over my dick this time," he said as he walked them to the railing, bending her over it before slipping his still rigid cock deep inside her.

He began pumping instantly, moving fast in and out of her, gripping her breasts while he moved. Tara could see the waves out ahead, heard them rising and crashing against the sand as Jackson moved inside of her. She loved every second of this rough taking, every thrust that felt like he might push through her completely. When he smacked her ass, she gasped, the sting sending trickles of desire so potent her pussy pulsated.

There was another smack, and deep thrusts, while her breasts gyrated with his persistent motion. She held on to the railing, her knuckles whitening. They were on his porch, in broad daylight, out where anyone walking along the beach could see them, anyone sailing by could look to shore and witness them fucking like wild animals. And she absolutely loved every minute of the freedom and the uninhibited pleasure. So much so she turned to look at him over her shoulder. "More," she shouted. "More!"

As promised, Jack gave her exactly what she wanted, pressing his palm to the base of her back and spreading her legs wider. She was so wet, the tapping of his balls against her clit driving her so wild as she pumped along with him that Tara wanted to scream out with delight. Instead, she did as he'd told her and came all over his dick and all down her shaking thighs. She came until she felt dizzy and he had to wrap his arms around her waist to keep her steady.

His release came almost instantaneously with hers and he moaned into her ear as he leaned over her. "Naughty Tara, what are you doing to me?"

Jack held her close to him as she slept. It was early evening on a Saturday and he was in bed with a woman, not sleeping and not having sex, but not wanting to get up either. He had a deal in play and didn't give a damn about working out last minute kinks or pushing the opponent's buttons to hurry the deal along. There was also a lunatic woman dishing out empty threats and then hiding in the shadows, waiting for who knew what to pull her final move.

And he just didn't care. He didn't want to move from this spot. She fit so perfectly in his embrace, her head cradled just beneath his chin, her butt curved into his groin. Her hair smelled like candy, its soft strands tickling his face whenever she moved.

He didn't want to let her go. Ever.

That was a powerful thought for a man like Jackson. Yet it was one he could work with. He could keep Tara in his life and nothing had to change. In fact, it would probably make things better. If Soleil's threat was to expose his connection to The Corporation, let her go ahead and try it. With a steady girlfriend on his arms, who would believe her? Or better yet, who would give a damn?

The documented owners of The Corporation were three Caribbean entities that trickled down to a line of other companies before reaching any individually named parties. The identity of the board of directors was not public knowledge since the business had been formed in the Caribbean. There was no way she could trace it back to him. And yet, he still felt like this was the threat she planned to use.

Jack had no other choice but to beat Soleil to the punch. As soon as they returned to town he would take Tara out again, publicly, letting the press get pictures of him with her this time. Then, he would introduce her to his parents. Going on the defensive was a strategic move against Soleil. Keeping Tara by his side and in his bed was turning out to be not just a deep-seated desire, but a necessity.

It was a great plan, one he felt pride in as he kissed the top of Tara's head again. He'd just inhaled, letting the scent of her hair ruffle his senses and strangely enough make his dick go hard, when he heard the glass shattering.

That whoring bitch!

His mind roared, his temples throbbing with the incessant headaches that had grown more intense in the last year. For a moment his vision had blurred as he looked through the lens of his binoculars, staring at the deck of that beach house. His stomach roiled at the sights before him.

She was down on her knees, her mouth covering that no-good bastard that thought he owned the world simply because he was rich. He'd slammed his palms on the steering wheel, the binoculars falling onto the floor as his entire body shook with rage.

He could kill her right now, wanted desperately to feel the warmth of her blood slipping over his hands, down his arms. His breathing had been coming in heavy, labored pants, but the thought of her bleeding, wounded and looking up at him with a plea to live in her eyes brought about a painful calm.

Reaching over to the glove compartment, he found the knife he kept with him at all times—the one he knew would at some point rip through her soft skin as easily as if slicing butter. Without another thought he opened the car door and stepped outside. Behind him the sea roared as angrily as he felt.

He hated her and Jackson Carrington, the arrogant bastard who thought he had it all. Well, if anybody knew that simply thinking something did not bring it to fruition, it was him. He'd thought one day he'd find some release from the torture that was his life, that if he'd just be patient, he would at some point get all that he deserved. That had been one big fat lie!

Reality had smacked him in the face first with the diagnosis of the fucking tumor that lived inside his brain. Months later, the same authenticity of life and how it could kick you in the balls at any minute was personified when she looked right through him, as if he was nothing, nobody. All the people she'd watched having sex, all the times she'd masturbated to something she'd seen on the streets or through her damned telescope, and she hadn't so much as stared longingly at him.

Stupid bitch!

Penelli had ordered her death months ago and the bounty on her head just kept rising. Putting away Big Mel, who as it turned out was actually Penelli's son from some prostitute he'd knocked up during his early days in the family, had hit a personal nerve with the mob boss. To say he wanted revenge was an understatement.

To say now was the time for everybody to seek retaliation on this irritating, lying, betraying cunt was speaking the absolute truth!

He took off at a run, fingers clenching the knife tightly. The house was only a few feet away. He'd parked just beyond a copse of trees located on the open property. He'd thought a man with Carrington's stature would live behind security gates and whatnot, but the arrogant bastard was right out in the open, daring anybody to have the balls to walk right up to him. Well, today was going to be Carrington's lucky day.

The house was so close, his destiny so near to fruition. He could hear that rutting bastard moaning as she sucked every drop of his come and had been prepared to kick up the pace, to run harder and faster. He'd stick his knife in that rich bastard's chest first, and then he'd cut off the very balls that she'd been toying with. She would watch in stunned, horrific silence wondering why her, why again. The blood splatter would be much more than there had been at Jana's crime scene. He'd slice that pretty motherfucker until his own mother would have a hard time identifying his body. And then he'd turn to her, see the frozen panic on her face.

He'd kiss her first. Every night when he lay in bed he thought about kissing her. She would love the way he kissed her, the way he touched her. She wouldn't be able to look away from him then. And if she did...when she did, he'd run that blade right across her pretty little neck. Slow at first, just enough to cut off any words she might want to say, and start a pretty flow of her blood down her gorgeous body. Yes, she'd have to be naked. He loved to see her naked. He loved to watch her just as she loved to watch others. He'd been doing it so long, enjoying every curve of her body for what seemed like forever. Now was the time. Now was for him. It was for...

He fell back against the ground, wheezing as he experienced a blow so hard he thought a tree trunk might have crashed into his chest. Then he was being pulled away, dragged as if he weren't worth a dime. As if all he'd done in his life, everything he'd ever achieved, hadn't been worth a damn.

CHAPTER ELEVEN

"Trouble in paradise?" Soleil asked in her throaty voice as she waltzed into the living room of Jack's cabin as if invited.

Jack was sitting on the couch, his arm draped protectively over Tara's shoulders. They were both fully dressed now after the breaking glass had awakened them. It had been an hour since the police had arrived and the uniformed officers were just wrapping up their investigation of the property. He'd called Trent Donovan before dialing 911 and was thankful beyond belief that the investigator wasn't away on assignment, but was in L.A. following up on the sedan situation personally for Jack. He'd vowed to be at the cabin as soon as possible. Since Jack had no idea exactly where Trent was, he couldn't predict when he would arrive, but felt better knowing he was on his way.

On the other hand, watching the tall, leggy blonde saunter into his personal space did not sit well with him.

He stood, moving so that he was blocking Tara from Soleil's view. His first instinct since coming down the steps to see the thick wooden handled knife with its long curving blade that had been thrown through the window in the middle of his floor had been to keep

Tara from any type of harm. Attached to the knife had been two pictures tied together with fishing wire; one of Jerald, Jack and Jason at a charity function a couple months ago and the other of Jack and Tara, staring at themselves through the mirrors above Jack's bed at The Corporation.

"What the hell are you doing here?" he asked, inhaling deeply to keep his calm.

She cocked her head, long fluffy curls tilting to the side, diamond studs glittering at her ears. "Nice to see you too," she quipped. "And who do we have here?"

Of course she'd seen Tara sitting there and of course she would immediately address that issue. Taunting other women with her startling beauty and practiced poise was one of Soleil's specialties. Her other attributes were more rumor to Jack than firsthand experience, of which he was thankful for.

"I asked you a question," he told her, taking a step forward. "This is private property and you are trespassing."

"Looks like you've had more than one trespasser today, sweetie," she crooned.

"Yes, it looks that way." He was right in front of her now, staring into her flint gray eyes, ignoring the perfectly applied makeup that gave her a flawlessly chic look and the expensive floral scent that surrounded her as if she'd taken a bath in the perfume.

"And isn't it a coincidence that you would show up shortly after someone breaks my patio windows," he said through clenched teeth.

She had the audacity to lift a hand, flattening her palm against his chest. "Down, boy," she said with a smile. "Did you forget my father owns the property next door? We're neighbors, remember. And when a neighbor is in trouble, it's the other's civil responsibility to come over to offer any help."

"You had no idea I was here," he said.

"To the contrary," she replied, tossing her head back so that her hair fell behind her. "I saw you drive in after I received a very strange message from my father regarding your lunch date yesterday."

Jack frowned. "I told him to tell you to call me."

She flashed a beaming smile. "I came over in person instead. Now, who is she and why are you hiding her?"

"I'm not hiding," Tara said from behind Jack.

When he didn't move she stepped to the side, coming up to stand right next to him, looking directly at Soleil.

"I'm Tara Sullivan. And you are?"

Soleil looked a little surprised at Tara's tone, but quickly rebounded with another high voltage smile.

"I'm Soleil Ducovney, of Ducovney Jewels," she announced.

Tara, to her credit and to Jack's amusement, did not look at all impressed.

"Nice of you to come over to check on Jack," she stated. "The police are almost finished. I'll see if they need anything else." Tara looked to Jack briefly before walking away.

He wanted to grab her, to keep her with him because she didn't look like herself. Sure, she was still beautiful and sexy as hell and the memory of their tryst on the back porch was still vivid and arousing in his mind. But her demeanor had changed. He'd instructed her to wait upstairs while he checked out what happened. The loud gasp from behind as he'd knelt down to get a closer look at the knife and pictures said she hadn't obeyed him.

Jack would never forget the stark fear that seemed to radiate through her body, the wild rise and fall of her chest and the tears that welled in her eyes as she looked at the knife on the floor. He'd tried to assure her that everything was okay, that he wouldn't let anything happen to her, but she hadn't seemed to hear him. By the time he'd crossed the room to take her in his arms, she was shaking all over and not saying a word. In fact, the first time she'd spoken had been when the police arrived and asked her name. The second time had been just now as she'd calmly introduced herself to Soleil.

"Not usually your type," Soleil said to him. "A little on the dowdy side, wouldn't you say?"

"I'd say it's time for you to go," was his immediate reply. "And when I say go I mean go far, far away. No more threats to my brothers or my family, no more of your bullshit. Do I make myself clear?"

She raised a brow, folding her arms over her chest. "Why Mr. Carrington, that's not very neighborly of you. I came to offer help and you're putting me out."

"I'm telling you that I'm not in the mood for your games. Whatever that phone call to Jerald was about, it stops now."

"Don't you want to know what Carrington secrets I might spill?"

Hadn't he just been thinking of that very thing? Before the window break he'd decided how to handle her little blackmail attempt. Now, Jack simply didn't give a damn what she might tell or to whom. It was a strange feeling, one he thought may need more consideration. But at this moment he couldn't bring himself to care about anything but that look on Tara's face—the look that said this incident had struck a familiar chord.

"Nobody will believe anything you have to say," he told her. "And we're not about to give you any money to keep quiet. So it's better for everyone involved if you just stop this nonsense right now."

She walked closer, again, touching his chest, this time running a long pink painted nail down the center, stopping just shy of the buckle on his jeans.

"Aren't you afraid I'll tell about your membership at The Corporation and your penchant for deviant sex?"

Jack grabbed her wrist, squeezing it tighter than he meant to by the quick shriek of pain from her. "Aren't you afraid of what I'll do to you if you dare open your mouth?"

"Is there a problem here?" one of the officer's asked, walking slowly toward them.

The look of satisfaction on Soleil's face disappeared quickly when Jack told the officer, "She's trespassing. Please escort her out."

"Yes, sir," the officer replied, and then looked at Soleil. "Ma'am, if you could come with me."

"What? Didn't you see him assaulting me?" she cried.

"Ma'am, Mr. Carrington has asked that you be removed from his property."

The officer continued to speak calmly as he touched a hand to Soleil's elbow, attempting to quietly remove her from the scene.

"You sonofabitch!" she yelled back at Jack. "You're so smug and so superior, always in charge of everything, directing everyone. Well, I'm going to have the last laugh, just you wait and see!"

Jack looked away from her, not wanting to give her the pleasure of witnessing his dismay that he may still have to deal with her once and for all. When he looked up again, it was to see Tara staring down at the pictures closed in a plastic bag still sitting on the counter in the kitchen. She lifted her head, finding his gaze and holding it, sending waves of fear and worry straight at him, causing his fists to clench at his sides.

CHAPTER TWELVE

With her legs spread partially apart, head phones tight against her ears and smashing her already messy ponytail down even further, Tara focused her gaze and aimed. Through the safety glasses her vision was a little blurry. She wasn't sure if that was from the glasses themselves, or if she were so afraid and so damned tired of feeling that way that she'd begun to tear up again.

Saturday night had been a rude awakening. It was strange too because now that she thought back on it, finding the boiling rabbit on her stove on Friday should have been enough of a jolt to prove it was time to take matters into her own hands. Still, she'd thought she was safe with Jackson, thought that whoever was taunting her wouldn't have the guts to approach while Jackson was around. Obviously, the intimidating and formidable aura Jackson possessed was of no consequence to a killer.

She closed her eyes, her arms shaking as the image of that long bladed knife instantly appeared. The pictures attached held their own measure of fear as she took them to mean that (1) the killer seemed to be always watching her and (2) that he didn't mind killing Jackson and his family to get to her. Both made her sick. She flexed her fingers on the handle and trigger, opening them, closing them and repeating. Rolling her shoulders, she took in a deep breath, releasing it slowly and opening her eyes.

He was the bull's eye. The man wielding that long sharp knife, the man that wanted her as dead as he had wanted Jana—Fernando Penelli—even though she'd never done anything to harm him or his family. For that matter, neither had Jana. Throughout the trial the question of motive continued to rise. Why did Penelli order Jana killed? Did she know something about him or something he did? Tara didn't know and at this point wasn't sure it mattered. What was of foremost concern to her was staying alive and not running, not again.

Narrowing her eyes, she zoomed in on the head portion of the target, because when she shot the bastard that was following her and scaring the sanity out of her, she wanted to kill him. She wanted to finish this portion of her life once and for all.

Tara squeezed the trigger, her legs doing their best to hold her upward even after the force of the shot had her staggering backward. Dammit. She missed the head completely.

Repositioning herself, Tara tried again and again, determined to get him—whoever he was—before he could get her. That was her first and foremost goal this time around, to live.

Three hours later, she was riding in the backseat of the Rolls Royce she seemed to spend a great deal of the time in. Jackson had been adamant that Mercer was available to take her any and everywhere she needed to be. At first she'd argued the point, pressing for her independence, especially in this relationship that she wasn't sure had any real longevity. Then, as the fact that someone was following her began to take hold and the time spent with Jackson started to fill her with more confidence, more trust, she'd given in and accepted.

Emilio's question of whether or not she could trust Jackson remained in the back of her mind. She did not doubt the coincidence of the events. The trial had been over for weeks and then, after Big Mel had been convicted, the stalking began. It didn't make much sense. Why kill her now? Why not before she'd had a chance to put the man in jail? And why target Jackson too when they could have simply taken her out one night when she was alone at her house? Tara didn't begin to understand the mind of a killer or a gangster, or even an officer of the law. She simply did not know why any of this was happening to her.

When Mercer pulled up in front of her house, the first thing she noticed was the black SUV that both Emilio and Russ drove when they were working on her case. After days of traveling with Mercer, she had learned to sit still and wait for the man to come back and open the door for her. The first couple of times she hadn't, he'd frowned. Not a mean look like Russ, but certainly one of disappointment. She'd stopped then, feeling guilt over disappointing yet another person.

Emilio stepped out of the SUV at the same time, watching her from across the street. Tara didn't want to start an exchange with him in front of Mercer, so she simply thanked the driver and stepped onto the curb, heading towards her house. By the time she had the front door open, she could hear Emilio's steps following right behind her.

"You have your own driver now?" he asked, closing the door behind him, Vicious' barking almost drowning him out.

Tara had worn sweatpants and a tank top to the shooting range. Her hair was pulled back in a messy bundle. She set her bag on the couch and dropped down beside it, her legs and arms tired from standing in the same position for hours, her mind overwhelmed by all that was going on around her. If this conversation wasn't going to start with "we found the guy that's hunting you," then she really didn't think she had the energy to entertain it.

"I don't have a car," was her glib reply.

"So buy one," he quipped.

Her head jerked in his direction. He was dressed in slacks and a dress shirt, sans tie, as if he'd had somewhere special to go today and ended up here. "Do you have any news for me?" she asked, her irritation clear.

"Actually, I do. It's really important too."

She sat back in the chair. "And Russ isn't here to glower at me while you tell me what's going on now?

"He called out, said something about a bad headache."

"Probably from frowning all the time," Tara said absently, rubbing Vicious' smooth white fur as her adoring puppy sat in her lap. She wasn't looking at Emilio anymore because she didn't like the way he'd been staring at her, as if once again, she'd done something he didn't approve of.

"How well do you know Jackson Carrington?" he asked pointedly.

She still didn't look up. He hadn't moved from the spot near the door where he'd stood after coming in. His hands had slipped into his pockets and his legs were slightly spread, reminding her of her own stance at the shooting range.

"Do you really want to know if I'm sleeping with him?" she asked instead, more than a little offended at his tone. At the same time his question made her nervous, her hand stilling on Vicious' head.

"I want to know if you knew Soleil Ducovney, the jewelry heiress with a reputation for connecting with rich men, was also having dealings with him."

She swallowed, lifting her head slowly to look at him. "I met Soleil over the weekend at Jackson's cabin."

"So he's sleeping with both of you and you're in agreement with that?"

"Go to hell!" she shouted, bolting up out of the chair so fast, Vicious yelped at being pushed to the side. Her heart was thumping wildly by that point, her angry gaze glued to Emilio's cool blue one. He looked as if he believed every word of what he'd just said. That because she was a voyeur, participating in a ménage would be the logical next step. Ignorant bastard!

"She's blackmailing him you know," he continued as if he hadn't heard her protest, or didn't give a damn. Both instances pissed her off further. "That means there's something in Carrington's past that he doesn't want to become public knowledge. Any idea what that is?"

"His secrets. His business," she quipped. "And I'm not going to let you stand in my house and insult me."

Emilio sighed heavily, pulling a hand from his pocket to run through his hair. It seemed this situation, or she in particular, was frustrating him.

"I'm not trying to insult you, Tara. I'm trying to help you. That's all I've ever wanted to do, was help you."

"You did your job," she replied, wanting desperately to ignore the tinge of compassion she heard in his voice. Emilio had always been on her side, always fighting for things the FBI did not want to do for her. That knowledge only cemented his former words in her mind. He was trying to help her. But at the same time he was questioning her relationship with Jackson.

"Look, for what it's worth, I'm not afraid when I'm with Jackson," she admitted, not able to speak to the trust issue, but not willing to totally throw shade on their relationship.

"Really? Someone throwing a knife through the window isn't enough to scare you? What else do you need, to be stabbed while you're asleep?"

The last words had her gasping and she lifted a hand to her neck to calm the flutters going through her. Vicious stood on the chair, body stiff as she growled. "How did you know about the knife?" Tara asked after a few seconds of simply staring at Emilio.

His lips thinned, his brow creasing. "Alright, you know Russ has been following you. He called me yesterday morning and told me everything that happened in Big Sur. I got a copy of the police report and immediately started looking into Jackson Carrington's background."

"Russ was in Big Sur?" she asked slowly.

"He's looking out for you too, Tara. This was a big case you testified in. Penelli's a mean ass motherfucker who will stop at nothing to get his revenge."

She nodded slowly. "Right. I know this. You've told me over and over again. What you haven't told me is why he would still want me dead after I've already testified and why the FBI is still approving of this marshal detail if I've already done my civic duty?"

Emilio paused, searching for something to say. But there was really nothing. No logical explanation, and that scared her even more.

"He's not going to stop until he kills me," she said quietly.

"And I'm not going to let him touch a hair on your head," Emilio vowed.

"I just want this to end," she admitted. "I just want the life I'm supposed to have. Why is that so difficult? Why can't I just live my life and be left alone?"

Tears filled her eyes, unexpectedly. She breathed faster in an effort to hold them back, but it was futile.

They dripped from her lids, rolling down her cheeks, her hands trembling at her sides.

Emilio came to her then, wrapping his long arms around her and pulling her close. His cologne was strong and burned her nose, but she was grateful for his strength and the comfort of someone who was on her side. She accepted the hug, wrapping her arms around his waist, letting more tears fall. They'd been through so much together. How could she be angry with him for questioning the new man in her life, the changes that had come so quickly after the trial? She should have maybe questioned them too, but deep down inside she knew she could trust Jackson. No way was he the one trying to hurt her.

The question still remained: Who was?

Otis Larring, the bodyguard Jack hired to watch after Tara after Saturday's incident, had just called, informing Jack that a man had been to Tara's house. Sitting in his office, he leaned back in the chair, contemplating all that was going on. Jack wasn't a jealous man, had never had any reason to be. He always got what he wanted, no matter what.

If it was a woman, he had her, and when he was finished with her, she was gone. Business, he made the deal. If he couldn't, he found someone who could work as a third party until it happened. There was nothing he couldn't buy or obtain, no wanting or needing ever affected him throughout his entire life.

Until Tara Sullivan.

From the moment he saw her, he knew he needed to have her. Like a forbidden drug she'd waltzed into his life granting him one taste and rendering him totally addicted. Now he had her. The fate of his life would continue on in familiar fashion, right?

Wrong.

A U.S. Marshal car had been following him. Why?

A knife with two pictures attached had been thrown into his window. Why?

Soleil? He'd been thinking of that all morning. Was Soleil really that crazy to try and intimidate him that way? He didn't think so. Then again, she'd shown up at his cabin directly after the incident, looking as if she knew something.

Now he had his driver taking Tara anywhere she wanted to go and a bodyguard on retainer to stay out of sight so as not to upset her, but to also stop any harm from coming to her. His mind wasn't on business, nor was it on the woman who could potentially destroy all his family had worked for. It was on Tara Sullivan.

He was frowning when the buzz of his desk phone sounded throughout the office.

"Yes?" he replied gruffly.

"Trent Donovan is here to see you."

Jack immediately sat up straighter in his chair. "Send him in," he told DeMarco.

"Yes sir."

In the next few seconds, Trent was walking through the door. Years after his last official military assignment, the man still looked like he'd walked straight off the battlefield, wearing black cargo pants and boots and a black t-shirt displaying his bulky biceps.

"Brace yourself," Trent told him as he approached the desk, taking a seat in one of the guest chairs across from it.

Jack leaned forward, his elbows resting on the desk, attention wholly focused on the man who obviously had news for him. One thing he'd always respected and admired about Trent was that he was no nonsense, getting right to the point at all times and taking whatever action was necessary afterwards. Jack nodded for him to continue.

"Her real name is Melanie Morgan. That's why Tara Sullivan had no history before coming to Seal Beach a year ago."

Jack's stomach turned, but he remained silent, positive that Trent was not finished.

"She was the star witness in the murder trial of Melvin Corone, illegitimate son of Fernando Penelli, mob boss out of New York. Two days after Corone's arrest, Melanie disappeared, resurfacing a year later to testify at his trial where she put every nail there was in his coffin, sending him to federal prison for the rest of his life. That was almost four weeks ago.

"That sedan you saw tailing you was assigned to U.S. Marshal Russell Samuels. Melanie Morgan now known as Tara Sullivan has been his case for the last year. His job was to keep her alive until the trial, which seemed to have gone off without a hitch."

"So why's he following me now?" Jack asked, his temples throbbing as everything Trent said circled in his mind. Things were falling into place, so he didn't doubt the investigator's words. That didn't mean he had to like them.

"The real question I think you want to ask is why was that sedan also spotted in Big Sur this weekend?"

Trent held up a hand just as Jack was about to speak, before continuing.

"And while we're throwing out questions, we might as well toss in how I knew the sedan was in Big Sur. I got a text message from an unknown number with a picture of the sedan, then another of the license plate and then another of it parked in front of the house right next to yours, the one deeded to Winston Ducovney. I was looking into all of that when you called on Saturday."

"Shit!" Jack cursed, unable to restrain himself as he sat back with a thump in his chair. "Soleil's connected to the U.S. marshals and Tara's case."

"I'm still working on that part, but I don't think she's in that deep. My guess is she's been in the right place to see some key things at the right times. Hence her threats against you and your family recently. But this Penelli dude, he's not the type to play Soleil Ducovney's games. She would either be his or be dead, so she's playing another role here."

"And Tara's playing the role of witness with a new life," Jack said quietly, his thoughts zeroing in on the fear he'd noticed in her since day one. She always made comments about a new life, starting over, taking advantage of what she had been given. Now, he knew why.

"Well, she technically does have a new life. My guy in the FBI confirmed that Melanie Morgan went into the witness protection program. He couldn't confirm who she is now, but because we were in basic training together and his wife desperately wants a CK Davis originally designed gown, he gave me an address. It's the same address to the house that Tara Sullivan recently purchased."

Giving in to the throbbing pain, Jack massaged his temples, letting out a deep, slow breath before looking at Trent once more.

"Now what?" he asked.

Trent shrugged. "I was going to pose the same question to you. I've provided all this information. Now what do you plan to do with it?"

At almost nine o'clock that evening, Jack was still sitting in his office. After his meeting with Trent, he'd thrown himself into his work, studying the contracts for the RGA takeover with a zealousness that had been missing over the last few days. If he were absolutely honest, he'd trace the lack of interest back to the night he'd seen her at The Corporation. The night he'd thought was the best of his life was turning out to be something totally different.

Trent asked what he wanted to do with all the information he'd obtained, but Jack hadn't answered because he had no idea. Of course he'd wanted to know who was following him and why. Now he did. He'd known immediately that Tara was hiding something. The fact that she didn't say anything about their first meeting in New York had been a clear signal of that. Again, he now had the why behind that question as well.

She'd called him several times during the afternoon. He had not answered and he'd finally instructed DeMarco to inform her that he was in meetings all day and could not be disturbed. The calls had stopped and he'd relaxed minutely.

He had a tremendous headache that had been lurking since the moment Trent had come into his office. Squeezing the bridge of his nose had brought no relief, and he'd just taken a swallow from the bottled water on his desk when he heard the clicking of the door being opened. With all that had been going on, Jack looked up instantly, his left hand sliding down towards the lower right desk drawer where there was a box containing a gun he'd purchased years ago and had never needed. There was also a security buzzer beneath his desk, but Jack figured he'd feel a lot better with his own weapon in hand.

But as he watched with keen awareness the person walking into his office, Jack figured another type of protection might be needed.

"I tried to call you," she said, backing against the door until it closed. "DeMarco said you were going to be tied up in meetings all day. I figured the meetings would be over by now, so I took a chance on visiting."

After clicking the lock in place, she began walking towards his desk. She passed the extended length of the room, where there was a leather loveseat and two more guest chairs as well as a small table and bar in the corner. In her path was about 10 additional feet before another set of guest chairs and then his desk. She stopped at the chairs, looking at him expectantly.

"It's late. And you're still here. Mercer has been very helpful. He brought me here and told me how to get up to your office. DeMarco wasn't at his desk, which is a shame because I wanted to put a face to the voice I've heard so many times today."

She was talking a lot so he knew she was nervous.

"How did you know I would be here?" Jack asked, unable to keep his gaze from dropping from her face to the short black trench coat she wore belted tightly at her waist.

"I hoped," was her quiet reply.

Her hands shook slightly as they went to the belt, pulling it apart. "Have you ever hoped for anything, Jackson?"

At that exact moment, Jack hoped she was naked beneath the coat, but he didn't dare speak that. So much had happened since the last time he'd seen her that he couldn't help but look at her just a little differently this time. The attraction was still there, living and breathing between them like a wild beast, but she was not who he'd thought she was and Jack wasn't a hundred percent sure how he felt about that.

"What are you hoping for tonight, Tara? What do you want from me?"

He'd been wondering that all day. Why had she really come to The Corporation again, if she planned to forget she'd ever been there before? And why get involved with him, of all the people she could have selected?

Her head tilted slightly, silky tresses moving over her shoulder. Her makeup was softer tonight, long lashes highlighted by a golden sheen over her eyes, lips plump and glossed with a shade of pink he found absolutely irresistible.

"I'm hoping that you can make it all better. That I can slip into your arms once more and forget yesterday and today and..."

She'd let her hands drop to her sides as the belt was undone, the coat slipping open just enough so he could see skin. Luscious caramel toned skin at her midsection and long glorious legs. His dick hardened, but she had no way of knowing that. He didn't move a muscle, simply continued to stare, wondering why or how she came to be in his life...again?

"You want to forget?"

She nodded. "Yes. I do."

What did she want to forget? The murder she witnessed or the night she was at the club, or him? Obviously the latter wasn't an option since now she was touching the lapels of the coat, shrugging her shoulders and letting it slip down to the floor in a quick, breath-stealing whoosh.

Jack felt like clearing his throat, like sitting up straighter in his chair and grabbing on to some semblance of control where this woman was concerned. But that was not meant to be. Instead he swallowed hard, sliding a hand down his thigh to caress the throbbing length of his cock, his gaze slowly moving over her blessedly naked body.

"I need you to take me, Jackson. Right here and right now," she told him.

Jack watched the rise and fall of her chest as she tried to steady her breathing. He loved the up and down movement of her pert palm sized breasts, mouth-watering at the memory of how those taut nipples felt scraping along the pad of his tongue. He watched her walk around the desk, moving slowly as if she half expected him to tell her to go. His body was never going to allow him to say that, while his mind roared with more questions, more concerns.

Still he found himself turning in his chair, spreading his legs wider, and waited with bated breath while she stepped between them, whispering again, "I need you."

His hands were on her hips before he could think of a reason to stop them. He pulled her closer, inhaling deeply of her soft floral scent, pressing his face into her stomach. Closing his eyes, he tried to forget every word that Trent had said and every word Otis had reported about the guy going to visit her earlier today. Like her, he found himself wanting to forget.

He kissed her, a small chaste kiss right at her navel. She shivered, her palms flattening against the back of his head. His tongue snaked out, lathing the indentation, his chest heaving with the urge to take more.

"Say it again," he whispered over her now damp skin. "Tell me you need me again."

Her hands moved up and down the back of his head, a warm caress that sent trickles of heat down his spine.

"I need you, Jackson," she told him, her voice sounding more honest than Jackson thought he'd ever imagined while being with another person.

His tongue stroked along her stomach again and again, moving downward until he was breathing over the soft skin of her juncture. He loved that she was smooth here, loved the feel of his tongue moving through her slit unfettered. She pressed into him and he slid a hand down the back of her thigh, lifting her leg until her stiletto heels were digging into his leg. There was a brief second of pain that sent a jolt directly to his dick as he separated her folds and licked along the already dampened skin. She thrust into his mouth and he moaned over her sweetness.

When it just simply wasn't enough, he lifted her, turning in the chair so that he could set her on his desk. She moved to lean back and his head snapped up. He glared at her, saying, "No! Don't move!"

His command was loud and forceful and he didn't regret it. The look of pure pleasure on her face was his reward as she sat straight up, doing just as he instructed. Grabbing the backs of her thighs again, he lifted them until each sexy black shoe was planted on the arms of his chair. "Relax your legs," he told her, watching as she did as he instructed, feeling the immediate thumping of his heart as he looked down. She blossomed in front of him like a delightful flower, the plump, wet folds of her pussy opening, displaying the tightened bud of her clit and her seeping center that begged for his tongue once more.

Jack gorged himself, loving her scent as it riffled through his nose, the sound of her moans as they echoed throughout his office and the softness of her thighs when they rubbed against the side of his head.

"Can I...please?" she stammered. "Please?"

Jack's shoulders tightened and retracted, his mind circling around her words, elation bubbling around inside his chest.

"Come for me, sweetness. Come for me now."

He plunged his tongue deep inside her after the words and only had to wait another second before her body convulsed around him, her sweet nectar dripping into his mouth like a favored treat.

While she was still shaking with her release, her head tilted back, mouth open as she breathed through every tremble, Jack stood from his chair, using one hand to release his throbbing erection while the other

traced the line of her neck around to her nape so he
could pull her head up, her gaze on him.

"Take what you need," he instructed, stepping closer
and thrusting hard and fast into her.

Tara gasped initially, then wrapped her legs around
his waist, locking her ankles and doing exactly what he
said. Every thrust, she took. Every yank of the hair he'd
wrapped around his wrists, she accepted. When he bit
along the line of her jaw, she whispered his name, and
when he sucked her tongue deep into his mouth, she
shuddered.

Jack only knew her. He only tasted, only smelled,
only felt her walls wrapped warm and tight around him.
It was only Tara. And with a start, he realized it had
always been that way.

As if the thought alone had brought forth his release,
he held her close, burying his face in her hair as she
wrapped her arms tightly around him, breathing his
name yet again.

"Clean yourself up," Jack said pulling away from her
abruptly. "Mercer will be downstairs waiting for you."

He'd been adjusting his clothes as he walked away,
and Tara stared blankly for a few moments trying to
figure out what had just happened.

Of course, she remembered the part about her getting
into a car naked accept for a trench coat and coming to
his office building confessing her need of him. As she'd
expected because he'd told her it was so, he'd given her
exactly what she needed.

*I want to take care of you, Tara. Whatever you need
I will make sure you have.*

Those were his exact words and, up until this very
second, he'd completely abided by them. She'd
memorized those words in place of the Bible scriptures,
heard Jack's voice in her head now instead of Doris

Leigh's. He'd even almost erased all of Jana's words of advice, because with Jack, she was living the life that Jana had wanted for her, the one Tara had finally decided to take possession of herself.

After a long hot shower, her conversation with Emilio had replayed in her mind. He'd frightened and angered her. But one thing about that conversation remained true—she trusted Jackson and felt safe with him.

Unable to speak to him when she'd needed desperately to feel that comfort, she'd decided to visit him instead. It was an impulsive decision, a bold and courageous one and she'd been full of pride at taking that step.

Now, not so much.

That thought came with a pang deep in her chest as she heard him open and close his office door. He'd left her alone. To clean herself up and leave as he'd stated. The callous bastard!

Tears stung her eyes, but Tara refused to let them fall. It was her fault, just as things usually were. Only this time she wasn't going to wallow in the blame. Jackson Carrington had opened a door for her. He'd proven that she could be as sexually inhibited and free as Jana had tried so desperately to convince her she could. He'd also proven that, unlike what her mother had preached, sex could be good. It could be intense and life-changing and emotional and...it could break her heart. Just as it had broken Doris Leigh's.

Using a few tissues from his desk, Tara found herself once again doing as Jackson commanded. Minutes later she boarded the elevator and exited the building, climbing in the backseat of the car so Mercer could take her home.

But this would be the last time. She would send Mercer on his way and she would forget about Jackson

Carrington as he'd so carelessly seemed to disregard her.

CHAPTER THIRTEEN

Tara shouldn't have answered her phone. She should have simply ignored it and the person on the other end because he was a jackass!

And because she'd already showered again, had dinner and was in bed with Vicious curled on the pillow beside her. She was finished dealing with people for the day.

Yet, she answered anyway, closing her eyes and mentally preparing herself to curse Jackson Carrington, the arrogant, disrespectful...

"I'm at your door. Let me in," he said the moment she put the phone to her ear.

Damn. She hadn't bothered to verbally reply but disconnected the call and tossed her phone across the bed. For two seconds she debated what she should do, and then cursed, because she knew what she was going to do. Pushing the sheets aside, she climbed out of bed and was at the door when a very disgruntled Vicious came trotting beside her.

"I know, he was a jerk to me today. I should let him stand outside all night long," she said while opening her bedroom door and walking down the hallway towards the steps.

Vicious barked her response—she agreed.

"But then I'd feel like I was running from him and I'm not going to do that anymore." She turned on a lamp in the living room and paused to look back at Vicious. The dog hadn't replied to her new comment.

"He's not dangerous," Tara insisted, because Vicious was giving her a warning glare. After another silent moment, Tara cursed. She'd left her gun upstairs in her bedroom.

She headed for the dining room where there was a baseball bat beside her china cabinet. With it firmly in hand, she looked to Vicious again.

"If this isn't Jackson at the door, somebody's going to have one hell of a headache come morning."

Vicious wagged her tail, baring her teeth as she stayed close to Tara's right side. Bat in hand, dog at her side, Tara unlocked the front door, pulling it open slightly as she peeked outside.

"It's just me," Jackson said without moving to come inside.

Her faith in the fact that he wasn't dangerous was renewed. If he were here to kill her, wouldn't he have simply pushed through the door the moment she opened it? Hell, she had no idea. For the billionth time she admitted that she was no expert on hired killers. Thank the heavens.

Stepping back, she let him inside before quickly closing the door behind him. She hadn't thought to look outside to see if there were any other strange cars out there. Dammit. Then again, did she really want to know where the killer was at this exact moment? Before she could give that any real thought, she was whirling around at the sound of Jackson's heated question.

"Why didn't you tell me who you really were?" he yelled at her.

Slowly setting the bat against the wall, Tara followed him further into the living room, watching the tense stance of his body, the muscle ticking in his jaw. He was very angry. And she was caught.

"What are you talking about?"

She licked her lips, folding her arms over her chest, pulling the t-shirt she slept in up higher on her legs as she was gripping herself so tightly. Jackson faced her now, his dress shirt unbuttoned at the neck, dark slacks still accentuating his tapered waist. If not for the way his eyes were basically glaring at her, she would have been struck by how absolutely gorgeous he actually was.

"Don't play games with me," he replied. "I'm sick of the goddamn game. I asked you to trust me and you lied!"

On the outside, Tara was sure she looked calm and composed, while the inside flipped and flopped with dread. Vicious barked, but didn't go after Jackson. The dog had never tried to attack him, she thought absently. Vicious obviously didn't believe he was dangerous either. Maybe both of them were wrong. Maybe what they should have been afraid of all along was this exact moment, the second when the past she'd been forced to leave behind came crashing into the future she'd wanted desperately to believe in.

"I am not a liar," she replied.

"Then maybe Melanie Morgan was," he spat.

She nodded, gritting her teeth so hard she thought she might actually crack a few of them. How had he found out who she was? They'd said no one would ever find out. But Jackson Carrington wasn't just anyone. She'd known that from the first time she saw him at The Corporation. He was more man than she'd ever come across, more intimidating, more forceful, more alluring than she thought one man should ever be. And for just a moment there, she'd thought he was the one.

"You have no idea what you're talking about," she replied, still trying to keep it together. Falling apart in front of him was not an option. Hadn't she given him enough already? Hadn't she put herself so completely in his hands, taking his commands, following his lead so that she could feel that blissful pleasure that had eluded her all her life? Any more humiliation at this man's hands and she would be completely destroyed.

"You are Melanie Morgan, or at least you were until a year ago. You used to live in New York where I saw you for the first time at The Corporation in Manhattan. When I mentioned seeing you again, all you had to do was own up to it, to tell me who you were and all of this could have been avoided."

"All of what?"

"This!" he said in an explosive voice. He waved an arm between the two of them as if "this" was a real entity staring them down, watching to see what would happen next.

His chest moved up and down with the quickened rhythm of his breathing, his lips thinning as he watched her. Yes, he was angry. But why should he be?

Was he the one who had been mentally tortured all her life? Had he sustained an abuse far worse than if her mother had simply slapped her around a few times? Had he watched his best friend in the whole world be brutally murdered? Was his entire life uprooted and he forced to start all over again in a world as unfamiliar as if she'd been born anew?

Hell no!

In the seconds that he stood there, staring at her as if she had somehow wronged him, Tara lost it. Gone was the control, the confidence, the pride, everything she'd worked on this past year and everything she'd hated not having for most of her life. It all vanished, just like that. And all that was left was her—a 29-year-old woman who had endured her share of pain and betrayal and restriction. She was sick of being told what to do or how she should have done it. Tired of being on the receiving end of judgment and criticism. Her body shivered with the overload, her temples throbbing at the explosion bubbling to the surface.

At her sides she curled and released her fingers and Vicious growled.

"How could I tell you something I don't know?" she screamed back at him. "How do I introduce myself to someone who swore from the first moment they saw me that they knew me, knew everything I wanted, how I wanted it, when I wanted it! How do I compete with a dead person and live up to another dead person's expectations and put a killer behind bars and live a normal life? Do you know the answer to those questions, Jackson? Do you? Do you?"

Jackson looked startled, but Tara wasn't sure if it was at her tone or what she'd said.

"All you had to do was tell me who you really were," he said, his voice much calmer than it had been before.

Too bad calm was completely out the door in her mind. He'd come in here asking for a confrontation and, dammit, he was going to get one.

"And who do you think that is?" she asked, taking a step closer to him. "So you no doubt used your money and power to dig into my past and found out who I was a year ago, what I went through to get where I am right now. What? Not knowing every deep dark secret of the woman you've been fucking for the past weeks was too much for the fabulous Jackson Carrington? Should I have passed your critical and judgmental background check before or after you put your dick in my mouth?"

"That's not what I said," he replied through clenched teeth. "All I wanted was the truth."

"And what truth is that? The one where I'm pretty and docile and maybe presentable enough to run in your social circles? Or is it the one where I'm just as perverted and screwed up in the head as you are to walk into an establishment like The Corporation in the first place?"

She was in his face now, jabbing a finger into his chest because the rage soaring through every pore of her body had her shaking and ready for action.

"You aren't all that honest yourself, Jackson," she accused. "Do your rich and distinguished parents know their son is two seconds shy of being a dominant? Do they know you own a significant portion of stock in a sex club that brings in billions of dollars worldwide every year? Do they Jackson?"

He grabbed her wrist the moment his name fell from her lips again, pushing her back until she fell onto the couch, him on top of her. Vicious barked and barked, running alongside the chair.

"Shut up!" Jackson yelled, and the dog instantly went silent. Turning his attention back to Tara, he continued, "Damn you! It wasn't supposed to go this way! You weren't supposed to be here!"

Tara blinked back her surprise. Jackson's eyes had grown darker. His body was trembling atop hers as he spoke. And his voice, it wasn't the same. It wasn't controlled.

"I didn't come looking for you," she said. "I just wanted to be free."

"And I simply wanted you," he admitted. "Both times I saw you at the club I wanted you. In New York it was a strong punch of lust and then you were gone. I thought about you all the time, wanted to know why you left, where you went, who you ended up in bed with that night. And then you were here and I—"

"That wasn't me in New York," she told him quietly.

He lowered his forehead to hers, closing his eyes as his breath continued to come in quick pants. "Please, just stop with the lies."

She shook her head. "I'm not lying. It wasn't me." When he pulled back, looking at her closely, Tara sighed.

"It was my twin sister, Jana."

Jackson pulled back from her so quickly she might have thought she physically wounded him in some way. Tara sat up in her chair. She dragged her fingers through her hair, taking a deep breath, closing and reopening her eyes. Leaning forward, she patted Vicious' head, reassuring her dog that she was alright. She didn't look at Jackson, but she could feel his intense gaze resting on her like a weight.

"We were born to Doris Leigh Morgan on May the first, six months after the day Doris Leigh's husband walked out on her. Miranda and Melanie, that's what she named us. She never told us we were mistakes or that we ruined her life but she never let us forget how bad sex was and how sinful it would be to get involved with a man. My sister was 15 minutes older than me. She was more vivacious and stronger and prettier. She was everything I wasn't, always."

Hating the dejected sound of her voice, Tara cleared her throat before continuing. "We escaped Doris Leigh's diluted spiritual rantings by going to college in Dalton. There we decided we would no longer be Doris Leigh's sheltered and mentally abused girls. We would be free. Whenever we went out off-campus and guys asked our names, Miranda would say she was Jana and I was Tara. They were our alter egos, the part of us that could do whatever we wanted and not be judged or convicted, ever. As we grew older, Jana became a beautiful and seductive woman. She loved taking chances, loved walking on the wild side. She dated rich and handsome men, sexy bad boys and anybody that aroused her. She loved traveling and seeing different places and experiencing new things all the time. When she returned home, I was there, living in the house next door. Melanie Morgan, high school advisor by day and Tara, voyeur by night."

Shaking her head at the memory, Tara continued, "I was still ashamed, still caught in the web of embarrassment and recrimination for my desires and my needs. Jana tried to convince me I was being silly. She tried to teach me to be different." Tara sighed. "I guess I was a bad student."

Jackson remained silent and it began to unnerve her. So Tara turned to him then, hoping that if he weren't looking at her before, that he would now. "Jana's friend Melvin had the membership to The Corporation. She thought it would be a good idea if I went with them one night because there I wouldn't have to be ashamed or afraid. I could do whatever I wanted and there would be no one to say it was wrong or perverted or just gross. So I went. That's who you saw that night wearing the black dress. I was lurking in the shadows, watching, wearing a pink dress that Jana said would have all the men watching me. But you watched her instead."

He blinked slowly, still looking at her as if she may perhaps be lying again. She wasn't and so her gaze didn't waver. She simply waited.

"I kissed her," he said as simply as if he were stating the date. "It was hot and my body reacted instantly. But I stopped."

"Why?" she asked, unable to prevent the word from slipping out. "You said you were aroused. Why didn't you keep kissing her? Why didn't you have sex with her? Nobody would have cared. They would have kept on going, looking for someone to sleep with themselves," she told him.

"You wanted me to keep going because you wanted to watch. You lived vicariously through your twin sister?" he asked, looking as if he were trying the words out to see if they sounded true.

Tara nodded, reconciling with him that they were.

"I stopped because there was nothing else besides the lust. She was beautiful and sexy as hell, but she wasn't happy and she wasn't…real," he confessed.

"Jana was everything," Tara insisted. She pushed back strands of hair, tucking them behind her ear. "She was courageous and sexy. Mel was livid that she'd walked away from him in the club. He'd had to take a phone call and when he came back she'd been gone. When he caught up with her he'd been so angry that he'd dragged her into the hallway, pressing her against the wall, where he took her until she screamed his name. We all left after that."

"So you got your chance to watch after all?"

He didn't sound disgusted by that realization, only sad.

She couldn't figure out why and she didn't want to. Her head was hurting, her chest heavy with the memory of her sister and all that they'd been through together. Standing from the chair she walked across the room, stopping at the window, flicking her finger through one of the closed blinds to see outside. There was nothing there but darkness, just like inside of her.

"When Melvin killed Jana I was devastated. I couldn't believe she was gone and I was ashamed that I'd watched her die only seconds after having an orgasm from watching her have sex. I was everything my mother predicted, everything she tried to pray out of me. Demented, perverted, scared and condemned."

"I think your mother may have been all those things at some point," she heard him say from behind her.

"I wanted to die myself," Tara quietly admitted, pain lodging in her throat, tears stinging her eyes. "I didn't want to live as Melanie or as Tara without Jana. I couldn't figure out how I would go on. And then the marshals came and told me I had to move on. I had to testify and I had to assume a new identity and start all over."

She turned then, surprised that Jackson had also stood from the couch and was only a step or so away from her.

"I spent a year convincing myself that I could be everything that Jana wanted me to be, that she'd died so that I could live. Ironic considering all the Bible verses Doris Leigh had us memorizing." She giggled nervously. "I don't have any mirrors in my house because each time I look into one I see Jana staring back at me."

A tear slipped free, rolling down her cheek as her body trembled.

"I went to court and I testified. I told everyone in that courtroom that I was a demented voyeur who watched a heinous killer stab her sister to death. They believed and despised me and convicted him of murder. I came back here and cried for the next three days. And then the marshals said they had to leave and I had to go on, alone."

Another tear and her shoulders jerked.

"I've been alone all my life. Even when Jana was there, I was alone. She was the spirit, the air, the sun and I was in the background, the fear. I tried to be better and yet here I am engulfed in the fear again, as if that's the one true thing that belongs to me."

"Stop it," he told her, moving until he stood directly in front of her. "Stop being the victim."

Tara shook her head. "No. I'm not the victim. That was Jana. I'm Tara Sullivan, the—"

Jackson covered her mouth with two fingers. "You're the one that I wanted the moment I saw you walk into The Corporation four weeks ago wearing a pink dress that stopped air from reaching my lungs. You're the one I kissed and felt the world around me tremble. You're the one I had to have, the one I searched for and investigated. You, Tara Sullivan, are the one I need."

The moment his lips touched hers again, everything inside Jack relaxed. He'd been tense since walking out of his office, leaving her there, sated but undoubtedly confused.

Trent had given him a wealth of information of which he'd barely digested before she'd come into his office so enticing and delicious. He hadn't been able to turn her away, hadn't wanted to entertain the thought that he could not be with her. And afterwards, he'd been ashamed.

How could he have considered walking away from her because of uncontrollable parts of her past? He'd wanted her to trust him, to tell him everything and to rely on him to take care of it all. Hadn't he told her as much when they'd first met? And yet, she hadn't. She'd been determined to live her life—this new life—on her own terms, being the person she wanted to be. Only now could Jack completely commend her for taking that stance. He'd been an overbearing and controlling fool and she'd been the strength that he needed, even though she didn't know it.

With his hands cupping her face, he kissed her slowly, letting his tongue make love to hers, pouring everything he had inside into her and hoping she would accept, hoping she would forgive. When her hands came up to grip his arms, her body melting into his, Jack breathed a sigh of relief. He pulled her closer, holding her so tight he was afraid she might break. "I need you," he whispered, pulling his mouth momentarily from hers. "I want you no matter what your name is or what you've done in your past."

Her hands flattened on his chest, her head lolling back as he kissed the line of her neck. "I want you even if it has to stay a secret."

"No secret," he vowed, pulling his mouth away and waiting until she was looking at him. "No more secrets. Agreed?"

She nodded, biting her bottom lip and lifting a hand to rub along his cheek. "No more secrets."

"Now that's settled, I need you naked. Now."

He was lifting her into his arms when she laughed. He stopped, looking down into her smiling face. "That's the first time I've ever heard you genuinely happy."

She leaned forward, kissed his chin and admitted, "This is the first time I've ever been genuinely happy. Thank you for that."

"No," Jack said kissing her slowly, deeply. "Thank you."

In the next 10 minutes Jack had Tara upstairs, in her bed, completely naked. He was naked as well and just about to climb on the bed and between her legs when she sat up, stopping him.

"My bed, my way," she said, her voice a husky whisper that raked along his dick like a warm tongue, causing it to jerk forward, eager and excited.

It wasn't what he was used to, wasn't the way their sexual exploits had gone these past few weeks, but Jack didn't give a damn.

"Your way," he acquiesced, following her lead as she pressed against his chest until he was laying on his back.

He watched as she climbed on top of him, her hair falling in curly tangles around her shoulders.

"I've wondered about this every night," she said, lifting a leg and placing a knee on the opposite side of his waist.

"Oh really?" he lifted his hands, touching the soft skin of her thighs as she knelt above him. "What have you wondered?"

"How deep you could go," she replied, positioning her center over his groin, using one hand to lift his throbbing erection.

"I've seen your length grow and thicken each time we're together. I've touched you, felt its growing heat and arousal," she spoke while rubbing her palm up and down his hard dick.

"And every time I come home and wonder how deep all of this can go inside of me. How much of you could I take at one time, how close we could actually become?"

Jack grit his teeth, her hand on his cock, her voice so sexy and inviting, her pussy so wet and ready the scent was teasing his nostrils. His body was drawn so tight he thought he might break any second now.

"Take me and find out," he replied. "Damn, I need you to take me now!" The words were foreign to him, the desperate plea unfamiliar. But none of that mattered. Right now there was only the need, the thick and heady spell she'd cast over him and the desire that threatened to stop his heart if she didn't continue.

She lifted her hips, guided the tip of his dick to her waiting center and stopped.

"Oh Jackson, how I've wanted you like this. I hope you're thinking of only me right now," she said, slowly working her pussy further down on his length.

He squeezed her thighs. "God yes, I'm thinking of only you, sweetness."

She slipped down further, undulating her hips as her walls continued to suck on him. "Say. My. Name," she told him, taking the last inches in, settling down so that the moisture from her lips dripped onto his sac, causing them to tighten even more.

"Tara," he groaned. "Your name is sweet, fucking fantastic Tara."

She smiled, placing her hands on his chest, whispering his name as she began to ride.

Jack grabbed her hips. He lifted his own, meeting every one of her thrusts. He watched her as she held her head back, her hair falling behind her like a sheet. Saw her mouth open with each gasp, close with every moan, felt her walls tighten, her pussy sucking at him and moaned his own pleasure. She was beautiful and she was courageous and she was everything Jack had ever wanted and thought he would never find.

She was the woman he could spend the rest of his life with, the woman he wanted above any and everything else. She was all his and he planned to make sure that she and everyone else in the world knew it.

When her release came, she bucked above him, arching her back and yelling her pleasure. Jack came with her, holding her hips down tightly on him as his own release came in thick jets, pulling every ounce of emotion he had inside free.

Finally free.

Half an hour later, Jack and Tara were just stepping out of the shower. He'd been watching her wrap a towel around her naked body.

"Stop looking at me like that. You've had enough for now," she said jokingly, obviously referencing the sex they'd had in her bed and then again against the wall in her too-tight-for- grown-people shower.

"We might as well get this clear now. I don't like limitations," he told her after tying his own towel around his waist.

He reached for her, pulling her body flush against his. "Especially not where you're concerned. I don't think I'll ever get enough of you."

She cuddled closer to him, a feeling Jack was beginning to think was the best sensation in the world.

"I might get used to that, and if you spoil me too soon, you're gonna have a hell of a time keeping me in the lifestyle I'm accustomed to."

Jack kissed her forehead, the tip of her nose and then her lips. "I'm going to give you the best lifestyle you could have ever imagined. Anything you want is yours, including me."

"Oh yeah," she said with a naughty smile. "I definitely want you."

She had just come up on her tiptoes to kiss him, her tongue slipping slowly into his mouth, when the lights went out.

CHAPTER FOURTEEN

"Bitch!"

Tara heard the word hissing through the air as Jackson pushed her behind him in the dark bathroom. Her entire body had gone tense the moment they were draped in darkness, dread wrapping around her tightly as she stood there knowing that this was it.

"You don't want to do this," Jackson yelled into the darkness. "It's not going to end the way you think."

It certainly wasn't, Tara thought instantly. She refused to die tonight, refused to let this bastard take anything else from her.

Jackson was moving now and she stepped right behind him, stifling a cry as her hip slammed into the side of the sink.

"You ready to die for a bitch?" the man's deep, gravelly voice sounded through the darkness.

He was in her bedroom. Tara frowned, heart slamming wildly against her chest.

"You ready to die period?" was Jackson's brave and intense reply.

His body was rigid, his steps sure as if he knew where he was going and what he was going to do once he got there. Of course that wasn't true because he'd never been in her bedroom before tonight and certainly not in the pitch blackness they were now in. Another issue was that they were both just about naked and had no weapons. Surely the killer, who sounded strangely like a bad Batman imitation, was armed as he clearly was dangerous.

Her gun was in a velvet bag beneath her bed, on the right side where she slept. Of course that was all the way across the room as they'd just made their way out of the bathroom, her bare feet sinking into the beige carpet after being on the cool tile floor. She'd just pressed closer to Jackson, one hand on his back, the other gripping his arm. Her plan was to whisper that she had a gun under the bed and to guide him in that direction, but in that second he grunted, falling to the floor, his body slipping from her hands.

She gasped, jumped back, and felt a gloved hand smack hard against her lips while an arm held her tightly at the waist.

"That's for having that rich bitch of yours hit me on the head out at the cabin. The silly whore is lucky I have bigger fish to fry than her conniving ass," she heard the intruder mumble just seconds before his voice grew louder.

"You stopped watching to fuck him!" The words were hot against her ear, the intruder breathing hard as he spoke them, holding her body so tight she couldn't reply even if she wanted to.

So many things speared through her mind at that moment, fear, fury, rage, anxiety. She wanted to act, to fight back, to make killing her the hardest task possible.

She squirmed in his arms, trying to get enough leverage to elbow him or lift a foot to kick back at him, but he was holding her too damned tightly.

"Oh no, Melanie, you're mine now. All fucking mine!" he taunted, his face pressing so close to hers she could imagine the contours of the ski mask he wore.

The gloves were leather, the scent making her nauseous as he pressed hard against her mouth. Since she couldn't talk and the last thing she wanted to give him was impression that he'd won, she shook her head as hard as she could, telling him she wasn't his, no matter what he said.

"Don't deny me!" he yelled. "Don't you fucking deny me again!"

He threw her down this time, her face thankfully falling onto her bed instead of the floor. She tried to roll over, to get to the other side of the bed to where her gun was, but a knee to her back stopped her.

"Keep still bitch! Dammit, I want to see you! What the hell's taking that generator so long?" he swore.

As if on his command, there was a flicker in the power and a rumbling noise. She had a backup generator in her back yard. The unit sat just beneath her bedroom window and it hummed as it worked to restore power. The light wasn't as bright as it had been, the generator only restoring a portion of power, but enough so that there was a dim glow in the room. Enough so that if she could turn over and grab the mask from his face, she could see who wanted her dead.

Who had the guts to come into her house and kill her…who…also knew her name was really Melanie…and that knew there was a generator that would eventually restore some power in her house.

Kicking out, she managed to turn over and had to hold the towel in place as her movements had it shifting down her chest. He was still over her, glaring down, a long bladed knife in his right hand.

"Coward!" she screamed, reaching up to grab at the mask.

He pulled back so that the material snapped against his face once more, not coming off the way she'd hoped, but twisting it a bit so that she could see a little more of his face through the eye slits.

"Stupid!" he yelled back, slapping her hard across the cheek.

Tara fell back with the force of the blow, closing her eyes to the millions of stinging pricks spreading up and down her face.

"No matter what I do for you, you don't appreciate it!"

He knew her and she knew him. The realization was subtle, like a blindfold had been lifted from only one of her eyes. In her mind she was running down the shortlist. Keep him talking, she thought Jana would say. Keep him talking until you figure it out.

"How do I appreciate it if I don't know who you are?" she quipped.

He was breathing heavily, standing at the foot of her bed dressed in all black, the mask crocked on his head, but only so much so that she could see more of his eyes.

"You know me! Just like I know you. I know everything about you and I wanted to make things better. After the murder I told you I would make it better. I told you," he said, lifting the arm holding the knife and pointing it at her.

Tara kept her legs closed tightly. She swallowed, trying desperately to calm her beating heart, to think and take the right action at the right time. Just as she'd said all along, this wasn't the same type of person who had killed Jana. That was quick and intentional. This was...she didn't really know...but something told her she had time—not much—but some time to maybe save herself and Jackson.

"You told me," she said slowly, staring up at him.

"Don't look at me like that!" He lifted both hands then, pressing the heel to his eyes. "Don't look at me like you feel sorry for me. I don't need your goddamned pity!"

His hands moved from his eyes, to the sides of his head. He shook it back and forth and Tara sat up on the bed.

"Then I won't pity you. If this is your way of getting my attention, it worked," she told him. "Just let me get dressed and we can go downstairs to talk about this." The words rolled off her tongue as if they were as natural as breathing. But nothing was natural here. This was a desperate situation. She felt it in the thick tension of the room, the straining of his voice, the shaking of the hand that held that knife.

Nervously she lifted her own hands, rubbing them down her hair and continuing to stare at him when all she really wanted was to get up and run the hell out of the room.

"You're not getting dressed. I want you just like that. I need to see you like that to do this," he told her, letting his hands fall to his sides. "Take off that towel."

"No!" was her immediate reply. She held tighter to the terry cloth material.

When he reached out a hand to her, Tara had to bite back a scream. He grabbed her by the hair, yanking her off the bed until she fell onto her knees in front of him.

"You're gonna do what I say, when I say now, no questions asked."

"Okay, okay!" she yelled at him frantically, her hands holding her up from falling flat on the floor. "Just tell me why. I have a right to know why you're doing this, why you want me dead."

"Arrrrghhh!"

It almost sounded like a roar as he yelled into the room. It also sounded painful, and she looked up immediately to see him once again holding his head.

"Let me help you," she said. "Tell me how I can help you." And then maybe he wouldn't have to kill her. Tara didn't know. She was working on instinct now. Saying whatever she thought she needed to say to buy time, to keep that knife as far away from her as possible. Whatever it took, she thought, taking another deep breath.

"You can't do shit for me bitch!" was his eventual reply, followed by his foot kicking out, landing in her stomach.

Tara rolled over in pain, tears burning her eyes.

"When I wanted you to look at me like that, you wouldn't! You sat in your room crying over a trifling ass whore who was either going to die from fucking too many men, or the knife that ended up killing her. She asked for every minute of that night. Did you know that? Miranda Morgan was a tramp and she messed with Penelli's money when she started sleeping with Big Mel. That's why she had to die."

She could hear him talking, hear him saying her sister's name, speaking about things she'd never known, things she had a hard time believing, all while trying to keep from vomiting on her bedroom floor.

"No," she whispered, curling into a fetal position as pain continued to roil through her midsection.

"Yes! That's why he ordered the hit on her. They didn't count on her perverted twin to be watching the entire murder take place and they never wanted you to testify," he finished, making that growling sound again.

From her spot on the floor she saw him lean over, placing his hands on his knees. She attempted to sit up, to get close enough. She wanted to see him, needed to know who this was.

He looked up then, catching her gaze. "I kept you alive," he said, his voice changing from the rasping it had been before.

It was clearer, more normal, more familiar.

"All these months I kept you alive. I let you live long enough to testify because I knew you needed that justice. But even after all that you still didn't look at me, you didn't see me and all that I'd done for you. If you'd just looked at me and realized I would have done anything for you, that I did do anything for you." He shook his head, closing his eyes, and then opening them again.

"I would have never contacted him. I would have never told him I could get rid of you for him. I don't need his fucking money! I needed you!"

Tara gasped at those words. Or maybe it was the way his arm extended so that the knife was only inches away from her face. No, it was more so because she recognized him in that instant. His voice, the words he'd said, his eyes...

"Emilio," she whispered. "Oh. My. God! What have you done?"

"No, bitch, what have you done?" he yelled back her, lifting until he was standing upright. "Or should I say what are you going to do?"

His free hand was moving over the button of his pants. She heard the rasp of his zipper and she shook her head, tears streaming down her face.

"No," she murmured. "No. No. No." It couldn't be him. He'd sat with her when everyone else had left. He'd listened to her when nobody wanted to hear what she had to say unless it was about the case. He'd rescued her. Dammit! He'd saved her not only from Penelli, but from herself. He'd made it possible for Tara Sullivan to live again.

"Get over here," he commanded. "I want you to suck me like you did him! Everything you did with him I want, because it should have been me! Do you hear me, bitch? It should have been me!"

"No" continued to ring throughout her mind. Emilio had been at Jackson's cabin, not Russ. That's how he'd known about the knife through the window and that crazy woman, the one he'd called Jackson's "rich bitch", Soleil Duovney. He'd been the one watching her all along. Everyday he'd looked at her as if he detested the fact that she liked to watch people have sex, and yet, he'd been doing the same. She couldn't move, couldn't bring herself to get closer to him, to the man that she'd trusted with her life and who would now end it all.

"Get the fuck over here!" he commanded again and Tara knew his patience was going. But after all she'd been through, so was hers.

His arms shook now. His fingers, hell, his entire body seemed to tremble. She figured he was in some type of pain, but didn't give a damn. It was all about her survival at this point, all about getting as far away from him as she possibly could! So she did move closer, she crawled near him, giving the impression that she would be sucking his dick in moments.

Eagerly he ripped the mask off, smirking down at her. "That's right, Melanie. I want you to look up at me while you suck me off! I want you to see exactly who's giving you pleasure, before giving you the death you deserve."

Heart beating so loud it almost drowned out his words, Tara lifted up slightly, his rigid cock jutting forward just a breath away from her face. She closed her eyes, saying a quick prayer before lifting her fist and punching him right in the balls. When Emilio yelled out in this pain, Tara didn't stop to look at him. She punched him again, watching as he fell to the floor, gasping for breath. Then she stood and was about to turn to get her gun when he grabbed her by the ankle. She kicked at him, trying to get his fingers from around her leg, and keep the towel in place at the same time. It was futile. He was too strong.

She yelled and screamed, hoping someone, anyone would hear her and would come to help. All the while she kept moving, kept twisting, until the gleam of the knife Emilio had dropped caught her eye. Rolling onto her stomach, she reached for it, feeling vindicated as she wrapped her fingers around the hilt. Then she was stabbing at her own ankle, praying she was chopping at his fingers and not her own flesh but working solely on adrenaline.

Emilio was screaming again, rolling over on the floor and finally releasing her. Tara didn't waste a second, but dropped the knife and got the hell up off that floor. She ran to the door and fell down the majority of the steps until she was in the living room. Face down on the floor, Tara didn't have time to catch her breath before she turned to see white and red.

"No!" she screamed. Coming up onto her knees she looked down at Vicious, who must have been down here ready to attack when Emilio came in. She probably hadn't heard her barking since she was in the shower with Jackson. Emilio had stabbed her, the bastard!

More than anything she wanted his ass dead now, but she quickly realized her gun and her cell phone were upstairs. Tara hurried into the kitchen, grabbing the phone and dialing 911. The moment she pushed that last digit and waited for the operator to pick up so she could scream "help!" into the receiver, her back door was kicked off its hinges and Russ appeared, gun in hand.

"Get down!" Russ yelled about two seconds too late.

Tara turned in time to see Emilio lunging for her, his blade sinking painfully into her shoulder before she could avoid him. Tara screamed in pain, falling back against the stove just as Russ rushed inside. The next thing she saw was Russ' big beefy hands grabbing Emilio's collar and pulling him away from her. The knife burned as it was ripped from her shoulder and Tara fell back against the stove. The room around her was moving, her vision blurry, pain searing through her body at a rapid pace.

Danger was still lurking. There was no denying that as she heard fists hitting flesh, dishes breaking, chairs falling to the floor. Emilio was trying to kill her. He'd knocked Jackson out and stabbed her dog. Hell, he'd stabbed her! Her head spun and she wanted to sink to the floor and sleep, to give in to the darkness that wanted so desperately to claim her. But she didn't, she couldn't.

She reached behind her, pulling the cast iron skillet from the stove, holding it in her right hand since the left shoulder was radiating with pain. She tried to steady herself, tried to focus, but could still only see the two men rolling around on the floor. One was Emilio, that's the one she wanted, the one she needed to focus on. She took a step on legs that wobbled way too much and slipped. Her back crashed onto the kitchen floor, her head slamming down with a thunk. Bells rang in her ears and her teeth chattered with the impact. But she still didn't give in. Turning her head to the side, she saw it, and knew that was her only hope.

Russ must have dropped his gun, deciding to beat the hell out of Emilio instead. She never would have guessed that Russ would be her savior, even though he'd always told her he was trying to protect her. It was his job, after all. Tara reached for that gun, grabbing it, not remembering a damn thing she'd been taught at her one gun range lesson. It didn't matter, she told herself. She only had one goal in mind. Coming to her feet, gun in her good hand, she aimed. The safety was off since

Russ had come in ready for battle. Now, she just needed him to move out of the way.

"Duck!" she yelled just as her finger was squeezing the trigger.

She had no idea where that first shot landed, but saw a big form moving from her line of fire. On the floor was the man in all black. Blood marred his face as Russ' fists had done one hell of a job on him. And those piercing blue eyes stared up at her.

"Don't let them take you there, Tara," Russ warned. "He's not worth it. That's why I dropped my weapon. No matter how much I want him dead, he's not worth ruining your life."

"You won't shoot me. You're a pervert and a whore just like your sister. You're not a killer," Emilio taunted, making everything Russ just said a moot point.

"And you're an asshole," she replied, pulling the trigger again. "A stupid, backstabbing, asshole."

Tara pulled the trigger until there were no more shots left. She stared into blue eyes that had long since lost their life, wanting them to close forever, to be gone from her vision, to disappear the way her sister had seemed to a year ago. She wanted him as bloody as Miranda had been, as still and as dead.

"He's gone," she heard someone saying and felt strong arms going around her. "You got him sweetheart. He's dead."

He'd touched her arm, his fingers sliding down the extended length until he could unwrap her fingers from the handle. "He's gone. You're safe now," he continued whispering in her ear. "You're safe."

Tara trembled all over, tears clouding her eyes just as the smell of gun residue and blood tickled her nose.

"You're safe."

She began to nod slowly. "He was going to kill me," she whispered.

"I know. But he didn't."

Her lips trembled now, tears streaming down her face. "He was after me all along," she said softly. The magnitude of what that meant still too incredulous to believe.

"I know, sweetness. I know."

"I'm safe now," she whispered. "I'm safe."

"Yes, Tara," Jackson assured her, shifting so that he could cradle her against his strong chest. "You are alive and you are safe. And this nightmare is finally over."

She lay her cheek against his chest, her shaking arms going around his waist, and finally closed her eyes. "I'm safe with you," she whispered before the darkness she'd craved only moments before took charge.

EPILOGUE

"What if they don't like me?" Tara said, standing in front of the two double white doors with gold beveled windows.

"They're going to love you," Jackson answered without hesitation. "Just like I do."

She stopped fidgeting long enough to look up into his eyes, to see the intensity and honesty on his face.

It had been three weeks since the incident. That's what Jackson liked to call it. In her mind Tara called it the salvation. Emilio Alvarez had come into her life offering her safety and a new beginning. He'd said everything she wanted to hear, provided all she hadn't been able to provide for herself. And then he'd betrayed her. Just as she had to figure her father had betrayed Doris Leigh.

He'd made her promises and he'd let her down. Doris Leigh had never recovered from that betrayal. Instead, she'd retreated into the Bible and poured all that hatred and disappointment she had into misconstrued words about faith and hope and love, systematically destroying a part of her daughters as well. Tara felt sorry for her now that she realized what her mother had gone through. She felt pity and relief that she would not walk down that same path.

Days after the event, when she'd felt strong enough, Tara had called Russ and requested a meeting. What she learned from him had been shocking and just a little more revealing to her. Emilio, on some demented level, had wanted her for himself. He'd wanted a part of her she hadn't yet known she'd possessed and would probably have never offered him. He'd also been diagnosed with an inoperable brain tumor, hence part of the reason he'd continued to work on her case. Three days after she'd testified, Emilio had been placed on disability leave from the U.S. Marshal Service after they'd discovered he only had a short time to live. That had freed up more time for him to stalk her.

Russ, the man she'd sworn hated her to the very core and she'd been guilty of despising on most days, had known something was wrong with Emilio. He'd watched him over the months they were guarding Tara and he'd sensed an unprofessional attachment to her. Not sure of whether or not Emilio's intentions were dangerous or simply out-of-line, Russ had used his personal time to watch Tara. He'd protected her up until the very end. She knew she would never be able to repay him for that kindness.

"I don't think he told Penelli about who you are now or where you're staying," Russ had said before leaving her that day they'd met in one of the conference rooms at Jackson's office.

"But you don't know for sure," she'd countered not really sure how she felt about that revelation.

"This is going to sound strange after all that's happened, but I believe Emilio really cared about you on a normal level, I mean. But that brain tumor, as it worsened, I think it started to distort his judgment. It changed him in ways I know he wouldn't have gone on his own."

"That's why you continued to watch me, wasn't it? You were not only doing your job, but being loyal to a sick friend," she said to him. She figured it was also why he—a trained U.S. Marshal—had dropped his gun in that kitchen instead of shooting Emilio himself. There was a glint of sorrow in Russ's eyes and for that moment, Tara shared his pain because she'd felt a similar type of helplessness as she'd watched her sister die.

"I've spoken to my supervisors," he'd continued. "We can put in for a special circumstances identity change, if you want. You would have to move and start over again."

Tara had immediately replied, "No. My name is Tara Sullivan and this is my home now. I'm no longer running away from the unknown. You said you didn't think Emilio told Penelli anything, then I'll trust your judgment."

A year ago she wouldn't have trusted anyone, let alone a man in law enforcement. But a year ago she wasn't Tara Sullivan and she didn't know the things she knew now. One of those things being that Russell Samuels would never really stop watching her. She could tell by the knowing way in which he'd nodded before saying goodbye and after all they'd been through together, Tara had felt comfort in knowing that.

As for Jana, or Miranda, as Tara had started to think of her sister, she'd made her choices, according to Russ. Good or bad, those choices set in motion a chain of events that nobody could have predicted. And Miranda Morgan's life went in the direction it was destined to. Just as Melanie Morgan's had.

"I didn't know," she whispered, and then cleared her throat because that probably wasn't the smartest thing to say at this moment.

Jackson smiled, touching his fingers lightly to her cheek. She loved when he did that.

"I didn't either," was his response. "At least not at first. As you know I didn't think it was possible."

"Love is always possible," she insisted. On a daily basis she reminded herself of that fact, just as she reminded herself that she had choices and that she could be whoever and whatever she wanted without caring if anyone judged her actions or decisions. It was her own therapy, the way she moved from one day to the next, smiling instead of crying.

Jackson nodded. "Because of you, I now know that's true."

Tara smiled at him. She couldn't help it. He was everything she'd never imagined she could have. A man of wealth and importance, of integrity and loyalty. He was handsome and caring, supportive and protective. And most importantly, he was different, just like her. He had struggled with sexual issues, just as she did, and he'd prevailed in his own way. She admired him that fact, even though she knew he still hated being dishonest with his family.

"I've never been in love before," she told him, touching the hand at her face with her own. "I never thought it was something I wanted. Until you."

"You are an amazing woman," he said stepping closer. "I'm honored to have you in my life."

He was honored. The words filtered through her like sunshine. "I love you, Jackson. I know it even though I've never felt it before."

She slipped his hand down to cover her heart, flattening hers over it. "I know it because you're in here. You're so much a part of me now that I not only need you, I feel like a part of me is actually you. That part we share when we're alone, when we watch each other, when you guide me to our joined release. That's love, I know it and I believe in it. I believe in you," she whispered, going up on tiptoe and kissing him. "I believe in you, Jackson Carrington."

Tara had immediately been accepted into the Carrington fold. Jackson had never doubted she would be.

After the incident at her house, they'd both been questioned at length by the FBI. They'd been bound to secrecy, not to protect the Bureau or the Marshals for their inadequacy in protecting her from one of their own, but to keep her safe from Penelli forever. Jackson and Tara had spoken at length about the mobster and the possibility of him still being after her. Tara seemed resigned to the situation and content to let the marshals handle it. Jackson, on the other hand, had immediately put security at the top of his list of things to do.

Thankfully, Tara's only compromise in dealing with the Penelli situation was agreeing to Jackson's offer to move into his condo with him. Mercer would continue to drive Tara and two armed guards were added to her security detail. She would work on building her company to possibly include a studio of her own at some point, while Jackson continued with is work. The key point was that they would be together and he would keep her safe even if he had to take a bullet for her himself.

Immediately following the incident, he and Tara had taken Vicious to a veterinarian where the puffy little ball of energy had undergone immediate surgery. The dog had settled into Jackson's condo as well as could be expected, but Tara made it perfectly clear that she did not want to live forever in his bachelor pad. She wanted a real home with constancy and warmth. Jack had promised she would have it soon.

For days they'd stayed in his condo, talking, loving, getting to know the two people they now were, the people who Jack now respected and cared deeply for.

Meanwhile, his brothers had been concerned because he hadn't gotten back to them about the Soleil situation and his father had worried because the RGA deal had been lost to a different buyer. To the Carringtons it looked as if the oldest son was in a crisis and they were immediately ready to jump in and help. In actuality, Jackson had been coming into the life he'd never known he wanted.

He and Tara had taken Vicious to a veterinarian where the puffy little ball of energy had undergone immediate surgery. For both their sanity and to keep Jack from hiring 24-hour guards on her—even though Russ had assured them there was no proof that Emilio had ever revealed her new identity to Penneli or his men–Tara had agreed to his offer to move in with him. She'd made it clear that she did not want to live forever in his bachelor pad, but wanted a real home with real constancy and warmth, and Jack had promised she would have it soon. For days they'd stayed in his condo, talking, loving, getting to know the two people they now were, the people who Jack now respected and cared deeply for.

Today, spending time with his family was the last piece to this transformation. As he watched his mother and Celise talking comfortably to Tara about designing a new website for Celise's restaurants, he'd known he was in the right place, doing the right thing, no matter what the consequences might be.

His father, Jason and Jerald were talking about basketball and whether or not Kobe needed to return to the Lakers when Jack stood up, moving to the center of the room.

"I have an announcement to make," he said loud enough to interrupt each conversation.

Lydia turned in attention first, a smile spreading quickly across her face.

"No, not that, Mom," he told her. "Although I can safely say now that what Jason and Celise have doesn't seem so out of the question as I originally thought."

He looked to Tara, and was warmed by her immediate smile and the slight blush that covered her cheeks.

"No, this is something different. It's something I never intended to tell any of you."

The room around him sobered, his father immediately going to stand by his mother's side. In that moment Jack admired that type of commitment, the love that held these two people together through any ups and downs. He could only hope that with all he and Tara had been through that one day they could stand side by side with that same type of promise.

"For years I've been an investor in a company," he began, looking at Jason and Jerald because he hated most that he hadn't been able to be completely honest with his brothers.

Jack continued. "It was a sex club where people could go...where I could go and achieve all the sexual pleasure that I wanted and needed. It was an intricate part of the man I had become and a secret I thought I had to keep from each of you, to protect you and our family name."

Jason said something under his breath, while Celise watched Jack earnestly. Lydia took her husband's hand as Jeffrey stared seriously at his oldest son.

"I know what you expected of me, Dad. I know what you felt I was meant to do for this family and I wanted to do all those things. I *did* all those things," Jack said, his shoulders squared, eyes focused on his father, on the man whom he'd tried so desperately to please all his life.

"But that does not change that I am a different man than you and possibly you two also," he said, gazing at his brothers. "I am not ashamed of that man or what he is because without that club, without the nights that I was there, I would have never met Tara. I would have never known what I believe is the love of my life."

Tara stood then, surprising him by coming to stand at his side, taking his hand in hers and looking up at him with as much love and loyalty as he thought he'd seen in his parents' eyes moments before.

"Last week I sold my stock in the club. Tara and I will be looking for a house and I will continue to run Carrington Enterprises. Only now, there will be no secrets. I have one life and I plan to live it the way I see fit, doing the work I love and being the man I am proud to be."

Tara squeezed his hand, and when he looked down at her she whispered, "I love you."

There was another second or so of silence before Lydia said, "Well, you were awfully rude to interrupt our conversation, Jack. But I'll forgive you. Now, Celise and Tara and I were about to discuss unique invitation designs for the Carrington Christmas party. If you'll excuse us, I'm sure you boys can entertain yourselves."

Before Jack could utter another word, Lydia was up out of her seat coming over to kiss her son on the cheek. "I'm proud of the man you are, son. Never forget that," she'd whispered in his ear before walking away.

Tara had just kissed him and moved from his side when Celise came up to give him a hug. "You're a good guy, Jack. I never doubted it for a minute."

Breathing a slight sigh of relief, Jack went to the bar to fix himself a much needed vodka, without the cranberry this time.

"So that's what you thought Soleil was planning to blackmail us with?" Jerald asked.

Until this moment, Jack had no idea his brothers had discussed the Soleil situation with his father, but since Jeffrey did not look at all surprised by the question, he was now sure.

"I thought she was going to go public with the news. Carrington Enterprises' stock might take a hit when it was known that the CEO had alternative sexual tendencies," Jack replied.

Jason held up a hand. "Let's just be perfectly clear," he told Jack. "I don't want to know what you like to do or how you like to do it. You're my brother and I love you and we can just stop the sharing right there."

Jeffrey chuckled. "I concur. Besides, that young lady you've got looks more than happy to be with you. So whatever it is you two do to keep that happiness going is fine by me."

When Jerald smiled as well, Jack finally relaxed, taking a swallow of his drink and at this very moment appreciating his family more than ever. "Deal."

"Now what do we do about this meddling little female that you boys have obviously pissed off?" Jeffrey asked.

"There's nothing to do," Jack told them. "I eliminated the threat. And now since I know she was the one who threw that knife through my window at the cabin and I've decided not to press charges, you could say I've got something to hold over her head should she try to come at us again."

"Do you think that will be enough to keep her quiet?" Jeffrey asked.

Jackson shrugged putting the glass to his lips once more.

"I don't know what it is she wants from us," Jason replied. "Is she that upset that none of us wanted her? I mean, damn, the woman has slept with a movie producer and princes for crying out loud. I know we're good men...good, rich, men, but she's taking rejection to a whole new level."

"She's a nutcase," Jerald finally surmised. "But she's barking up the wrong tree if she thinks she can blackmail anything out of us."

Sitting back in his chair, the middle Carrington brother, glanced at Jack. "You've been mighty busy these past few weeks, big brother. You fall in love, lose a big deal, and start house hunting. I hear you even have a dog now."

Jason laughed. "Yes, a white fluffy dog from the pictures Tara was showing Celise during dinner. Very cute for a man such as you, Jack."

"Whatever," was Jack's reply. "All I know is its working and I'm happy and I'm just going to take it from there."

Jeffrey got up from his seat then, crossing the room to join his oldest son at the bar. Clapping a hand on his shoulder, he said, "That's right, son. If you're happy, you go with it. That's all that matters in the end."

COMING JULY 2015

The final dangerously sexy installment to
The Carrington Chronicles

HAVING YOU

By A.C. Arthur

Available In Print & Ebook formats
The Carrington Chronicles
Wanting You
Needing You
Having You – *COMING July 2015*

Made in the USA
Las Vegas, NV
13 November 2024